The Wedding Dress

WHITE WEDDINGS
BOOK ONE

LILLY MIRREN

BLACK LAB PRESS

CHAPTER
One

"YOU ALWAYS MISUNDERSTAND ME," Kevin spat.

Amelia Wilson pressed both hands to her cheeks. "I don't know what to say. I'm sorry."

"You can't just apologise and expect it all to be okay."

"What do you want from me?" She sighed, feeling tired to her very bones. This fight was the same every time. He didn't like something about her, she didn't know what could be done to fix it, she fought back, he got angry, she apologised, and round and round they went.

Dappled light danced across the barn floor. In the distance, a horse neighed. Amelia raised a foot to rest on a hay bale while she tugged on her riding boots one at a time.

"I want you to care."

"I do care."

"I sometimes wonder if you have a heart. You're so cold and calculating. Look at you — you haven't even broken a sweat. I'm a mess, and you're absolutely fine."

She resisted the urge to roll her eyes. He hated when she did that. "I'm not sure what purpose it would serve for me to be all emotional."

"It would show that you care!" he exploded.

She didn't respond. These kinds of conversations always left her feeling the same way — empty, ashamed, alone. She wasn't like other people and didn't know what to do about it. They showed emotion, but she barely felt any most of the time. Anger was an emotion she was well acquainted with, but whatever this thing was that Kevin was experiencing, she just didn't get it. Why get so worked up over an argument they seemed to have every other week?

Dust tickled the inside of her nostrils, and she pressed a hand over her nose to stifle a sneeze. The dry heat was oppressive, but it did a number on her nasal passages. Her nose was constantly red, and her eyes itched. Not to mention the ever-present sunburn across her cheeks. The scents of hay and horse manure combined with the sweat of bodies and the stink of livestock, reminding Amelia of freedom. There was nothing she loved more than riding horses and being out on the land, away from everyone and everything. There was power in a woman and her horse riding alone, without needing anything from anyone.

"You're saying you want to move in together. Is that right?" She was doing her best to understand him, but sometimes he was so emotional and dramatic, she wondered if it was worth it.

He groaned. "I want to know where this relationship is headed. I'm not exactly the type who settles down, but we've been dating for five years and you still aren't ready to go to the next level. Even I'm getting itchy. I don't understand why you're not. Aren't you supposed to have a biological clock ticking or something like that?"

This time, her eye roll was perfectly justified, and anger fanned a flame inside her. "A biological clock? That's your argument for why I should move in with you? Very romantic, Kev."

"You know I'm not a sap. You also know how I feel about you."

"Do I?" She wasn't so sure about that. Sometimes she thought perhaps she was just arm candy for him to show off at the pub on the rare occasion when she joined him and his mates.

"You bloody well should. I've been here for five years. That's enough for most girls."

"I'm not most girls." Her stomach clenched. She didn't owe anyone anything. Why did he think he was entitled to take something from her? Especially since she wasn't sure it was something she could give. Maybe she wasn't capable of love. It would make sense, given her childhood. But Kevin had never understood that about her. He couldn't understand. He'd been raised by two loving parents and had four brothers and sisters he saw every week.

"That's the truth."

"What's that supposed to mean?"

He reached for her hand and held it between his, his tone softening. "I mean that you're one of a kind. You're amazing and sexy, but you drive me crazy. I don't know what you're thinking—I can't guess how you feel. You tell me nothing, give me no clues. And yet I let you keep tagging me along. I'm not sure this can go on for much longer, but I don't know what else to do. I'm head over heels for you."

She smiled. This was familiar territory. She hated it when he lost control of his emotions and took it out on her. But he was reverting back to his charming self, and she knew they could leave the argument alone for another week or two. But he was right about one thing. They couldn't keep living this way. She was sick of the arguing. The way he pushed her constantly to move in, or get engaged, or have a baby — any of those steps would be fine with him. He'd made it perfectly clear. Just so long as they were moving forward in their relationship. But she didn't want to do things out of order. Her own parents had done that, and look where it'd gotten them.

When she made the decision to live with a man and have a

family with him, it would be because she loved him and wanted to spend her life with him — and only after they were married. The commitment was what she was looking for. Yet not with Kevin. Even though on paper, he was perfect for her, there was something missing. She had no idea what it was, but she couldn't ignore the fact that she didn't feel about him the way he did about her. Although it did make her question whether she was even capable of those emotions, given the fact that she'd never loved anyone. Well, maybe her last foster mother and a few of her foster sisters. But that was a different kind of love, and not one she relied on.

She'd never been able to bring herself to break up with Kev. If she did that, she'd officially have no one in her life who cared about her. He was the only person in the entire world who wanted to spend his free time with her, who called her at the end of a long day to talk, who offered her some kind of stability, affection and companionship, no matter how temporary it might be.

Breaking up with him would sever her connection to the world of love and community she'd always wanted. And she couldn't do that. Maybe one day, but not yet.

She reached forward to kiss his lips. He pulled her closer and wrapped his arms around her to deepen the kiss. She didn't resist.

"Why do you do this to me?" he asked.

She shrugged. "I can't help who I am. You know this about me — I'm all messed up inside. I'd tell you more, but it's really boring."

"Maybe you should talk to someone."

"I saw a therapist a few years ago and talked all about feelings, it was utterly painful. And the one thing I learned is that it's going to take me time to overcome some of my issues. I don't trust people and I find intimacy difficult. At least, that's what the therapist said. I didn't keep seeing her, though, because she was expensive and I aged out of the system, so Medicare wouldn't cover any more sessions. But I got the general gist of things, I think."

"That's great, Milly, but I need an answer."

"All I'm saying is give me some time."

"I've given you five years of my life."

"And I've given you the same."

"That's true," he admitted. "Still, it doesn't change anything. Why won't you just accept that we're meant to be together?" He groaned and took a step back, running his fingers through his hair.

She reached for a horseback-riding helmet resting beside her on a bale of hay, pushed it onto her head and buckled it beneath her chin. "We can talk about it later. I've got to get to work or I'll lose my job. And then where would I be?"

"Maybe you'd finally have to rely on me," he muttered.

The idea of that sent a shiver through her body. She couldn't imagine allowing herself to be in a situation where she had to rely on anyone for her livelihood and safety ever again. She'd spent her entire childhood being ferried from one foster home to another, always at the whim of the adults who ran the system. She'd felt powerless for the first eighteen years of her life—she wasn't about to allow that to happen again.

"I'll see you tonight," she called, resisting the urge to snap at him, as she spun on her heel and headed out of the barn and into the glaring sunlight. Irritation buzzed up her spine. Why should she rely on him? He'd spent the past five years pointing out her flaws, threatening to leave. He wasn't someone she could rely on, yet he expected her to give up everything that made her who she was and mould herself to fit his view of how she should be.

"Bye," he said quietly behind her.

She didn't bother responding. Maybe it was time to move on. She didn't usually stay so long in one place and was getting irritable. It was her home, for now. But she'd spent five years in one place, Longreach, in the middle of the Queensland Outback. And she'd never intended to stay at all.

The wildness of the place, the hardness of the people, the promise of work with horses and livestock—it'd been too much for her wandering heart to pass up. So, she'd stayed. And then she'd met Kevin, and it made sense to stay longer. But the coast was calling her name. She'd never been away from the beach this long before. And with the way things were going between her and Kevin, it could be the perfect time to pack up and head east.

The horse she was set to break in stood waiting in a small, round yard. She watched it briefly. It was a young green stallion who'd been captured during a roundup of brumbies several months earlier. She guessed he was about three years old. And she'd had reservations about breaking the horse, but Bob, her boss, was adamant.

"If you can't do a simple break, Milly, what have we hired you for? Eh?" he'd said with an annoyed shake of his head, his half-moon glasses perched on a thin nose beneath a balding pate. "Get to it."

He'd gone back to staring at the computer screen at his small desk, and she'd headed out to the barn to prepare, where Kevin was looking for her. The interaction with her boyfriend had distracted her momentarily, and her head felt muddled.

What was she doing again? Oh, yeah. Looking for the bridle.

She strode back into the barn and found the bridle she'd used for several days now to get the brumby ready for her first attempt at riding him. She didn't want to rush things, but Bob had a schedule he wanted her to keep. There was already an interested buyer waiting, and if the horse was unbroken, that buyer would look elsewhere for their purchase.

She climbed over the fence and spoke quietly to the horse as she approached. His eyes were focused on her, and his ears flickered back and forth. A swish of the tail as she reached him, and his head jolted up suddenly. She soothed him with a stroke along his neck, and his head lowered again, eyes wide.

"Come on, good boy," she crooned as she slipped the bridle into place over his ears and adjusted the bit in his mouth.

His head jerked back a couple more times, but each time, she drew him back into a calm demeanour with her soft voice and gentle hands.

"Let's do this," she said. "Good boy. It's going to be fine. We're all going to be fine."

Nerves fluttered in her chest as she gathered the reins. He wasn't ready for a saddle yet, but she preferred to start things off bareback anyway. She had only broken two other horses, and both of them had already been hand raised and were easy to handle. This horse would be on another level entirely, but Bob believed she could do it. And she'd never know if she was prepared for a brumby stallion until she tried.

She hated that her boss was in such a rush. This horse was still so young and flighty. Another six months would give him time to mature and for her to win him over. But it was all about the money for Bob and the property owner. They didn't want to keep feeding brumbies if they could get them to the sale yard and make top dollar for them.

The station had been in drought for the past three years. There was barely a blade of grass on the ground, and feeding livestock was expensive. Red dust sifted through the railings of the fence that encircled her and the horse. The sun baked her shoulders beneath the checked long-sleeve shirt. Her long brown hair hung messy over one shoulder. It was the same colour as the bay horse beside her.

"Okay, boy, are you ready?" she asked.

The horse quivered beneath her fingers. Her stomach clenched, and her head felt light.

Carefully she slid onto the horse's back. He stood still, ears twitching. She smiled. "Good boy…"

As the words left her mouth, the horse rose on his hind legs into a rear, then bucked. She held on to the reins and a handful of mane, her legs wrapped firmly around his sides.

"Whoa!" she called.

But the brumby wasn't listening. He bucked again, over and over. Head down, he was doing everything he could to dislodge her, and she felt her grasp slipping.

Then she was sailing through the air. She readied herself to hit the ground, but it still knocked the wind out of her. She landed hard, on the top of her back, and heard a crack.

That's not good.

As she lay on her back, looking up at the washed-out sky overhead, she marvelled at how calm she felt. Nothing hurt too badly—maybe she'd be okay. She tried to sit up, but she found she couldn't move. Then the pain washed over her. It emanated from her neck, and it rushed up to her head, making her cry out.

"Milly!"

She heard Bob's voice in the distance. Then he was beside her, looking down with concern, his grey eyes bloodshot and his mouth ajar as he puffed thin, wheezing breaths.

"You okay?" he asked.

She tried to shake her head but couldn't. The pain was too great, and her body wasn't cooperating.

"Can't move," she said.

His eyes narrowed. "Don't try. Stay still. I'll call the ambos."

What followed was a blur of pain, panic, anger, denial and flashing lights. The ambulance took an hour to get to the remote station, and by that time, Bob had run through every conversation he could think of to keep her distracted and now sat quietly by her side holding her hand. She could feel his warm hands around hers, but she still couldn't feel her feet.

And she asked him a question he refused to answer over and over.

"What's wrong with my legs? Why can't I feel them?"

He'd pat her hand again and reply, "Don't worry about that right now. They'll be here as soon as they can. Then we'll get some answers."

She'd never seen Bob anxious before, and certainly never held his hand. But he was worried now—she saw it in his eyes. So she closed her own and tried her best to think of other things. The beach, the curling waves, jumping over the waves and catching them to shore. She thought of her time living with her last foster mother in Palm Beach and how it'd changed the direction of her life, having someone who finally seemed to care whether she ate, did her homework, or ditched to smoke behind the library. It bothered her to have rules, but at the same time, it gave her a sense of security she'd never had before, and now looking back, she could see how much Hannah had impacted her, even though she'd only taken her on at fifteen years of age.

Tears filled her eyes. What would Hannah say if Milly never got her legs working again? Milly had lost contact with her, hadn't called her in months. Leaving her past behind was the easiest way to pretend it never existed, but she shouldn't have let go of the one person who'd made that past bearable. She wouldn't do it again. If she made it out of there, she'd call Hannah and reconnect. She hadn't realised just how much she missed her, along with a few of the foster sisters who'd come and gone over the years and who'd been her lifeline during that lonely period of her life. She'd pushed them all away when she moved out of home and went on with her life. But now they were the people who sprang into her mind, who lingered in her thoughts, as she lay waiting for the ambulance to arrive.

The horse wandered by, reins dragging in the dust. Bob let go of her hand to walk him back out of the yard and release him into an adjoining field to graze on bales of scattered hay with the other horses.

Just then, the ambulance pulled into the yard. Milly heard the tyres crunching on the circular gravel drive. Bob spoke to them in a tone she recognised as concern, but she couldn't make out the words they exchanged.

The paramedics were chipper and loud when they spoke to her. But before she could answer, her thoughts grew foggy around the edges, and then she slipped into darkness.

CHAPTER
Two

THE ENTRANCE to the Rockhampton Police Complex on Bolster Street smelled of vape smoke and urine. Callum Montague's nose wrinkled as he stepped through the glass doors and into the reception area. It must've been a busy night — he was grateful to be finished with night shifts on the force.

"Morning," he called out to the woman sitting behind the bulletproof glass at the reception counter.

She greeted him in return, a telephone headset wrapped around her brown curls, flattening them in a loop behind her ears.

"Ready to leave the nest, Detective?" asked a voice behind him.

He spun around to see his best friend and newly appointed partner, Brad, following him through the doorway. Brad wore a button-down shirt, his sleeves rolled up, and a pair of charcoal dress pants. He'd always been the dapper one of the two.

Callum grinned. "Ready as I'll ever be, I suppose."

"We're gonna miss you around here."

"Thanks, Brad. I know we weren't partners for long, but it's been real."

"For sure," Brad replied. "And thanks to you, now I have to break in someone else."

Callum grunted. "You mean you've got to convince someone else that eating curry in the cruiser is a good thing and won't stink up the entire car?"

"Lesson number one," Brad replied with a wink. "My mum makes the best curry in town."

"That wouldn't be hard," Callum replied. "But you're right, it is good. It just doesn't smell good in my car."

"You'll get over it. And it's not your car anymore. It's mine."

"You can stink it up as much as you like now," Callum agreed.

Brad slapped him on the shoulder. "Good luck with everything. Now come inside so everyone can shout surprise at you and ruin your whole day."

Callum arched an eyebrow. "Seriously?"

"Sorry, mate. It's just got to be done."

Callum braced himself with a deep breath, then pushed his way through the door and into the office where he'd spent almost every day of the past ten years.

"Surprise!" The shout from the various staff who jumped out from behind cubicle walls and through doorways was louder than he'd expected.

There were poppers and noise makers, balloons and a cake. And by the time the party was over and everyone had shuffled back to their desks or out to follow leads and catch criminals, Callum was ready to leave. It'd been a difficult decision to walk away from the career he'd spent a decade building. But he couldn't face coming into work every day now, after everything that'd happened. And so, it was the only choice that made sense.

His boss had asked if he was depressed. He didn't think

he was—he still managed to get up each day and go for a run. He still lifted weights religiously. He still spent time with friends and enjoyed watching sports or bushwalking on his days off. But he'd lost his love for the job, and he didn't want to stay in Rockhampton any longer. There were ghosts around every corner, reminding him minute by minute of what he'd lost and what he could never get back.

He waved goodbye and tucked the small pile of gifts he'd received in the same box as the personal items from his desk. He carried the box under his arm and handed over his badge, gun and ID on his way out. Then he exhaled in relief as the glass doors swung shut behind him for the very last time.

He was moving south. Starting a new life. One that involved relaxing by the beach, avoiding criminals and enjoying the small pleasures of a normal, low-stress existence.

"Callum!" a feminine voice called out behind him.

He squeezed his eyes shut. *Almost got away.* Then he turned to face her. "Hi, Beth."

She jogged towards him, her navy uniform perfectly pressed, her cap pulled low over piercing blue eyes. "I tried to get a chance to talk to you inside, but you were avoiding me."

He didn't bother contradicting her. "What do you want, Beth? I'm on my way out."

Her eyes clouded with hurt. "I know you're leaving. I got the memo."

"There's no need to be snide. You know why I'm going."

"But that's just the thing, we could try again. I don't know why you won't talk to me about it." She laid a hand on his arm, and he stared at it a moment — her smooth red fingernails pressed into his shirt sleeve.

He tugged his arm away. "It's too late for all that. You're just having second thoughts because I'm leaving and you know you won't see me again. But the same issues exist between us now as they did then."

"What do you mean? You're not coming back at all? Not even for a visit?"

"Nope. There's nothing to bring me back to Rocky. My parents moved south, my partner is dead and you ended our engagement. Why would I visit?" She always was the type to want her cake and eat it too. She hated not to have him in her life, but she clearly didn't want to be his fiancée anymore. He knew she'd prefer to keep things casual, but that wasn't something he was willing to do now that he was in his thirties. He wanted to find someone who loved him enough to commit their life to him, not just good times together on a Saturday night.

"You have friends here, like Brad. You know that. Me included."

"You're not my friend, Beth. You never were. We were going to spend our lives together, but you broke it off because you wanted to have a fling with some guy you met at a concert. Fine with me—it showed me just who you really were before it was too late. I'm grateful to you, honestly I am. I don't hold anything against you. We weren't right for each other, and you saw that before I did. I think I knew it too, but I wasn't ready to admit it to myself. Now I am ready. So, let's both move on — no hard feelings."

She pouted and pressed her hands to her slim hips. "I apologised for that."

"And I accepted your apology." He waved a hand in the air. "It's all for the best. Let's forget about it."

Her eyes narrowed. "Don't you love me anymore?"

He studied her pretty face, smattered with tiny freckles across her nose. There was a time when he would've hung the stars for her, but now he didn't feel anything but pain when he looked at her. "No, I don't."

She gaped. "That's a horrible thing to say. We were engaged only a few months ago."

"You pushed me to propose, and I did it because I wanted

to make you happy. I'm sorry, but I should never have asked you to marry me when I wasn't sure."

She chewed the inside of her cheek. "What will you do?"

"I've been studying personal training part-time on my days off for years. I did it for enjoyment, to understand the body better and help me with my workouts, but now I'm thinking it might be a career for me. I finished the last subject a few days ago, and I'm just waiting for my graduation certificate."

"You're willing to leave the force behind and become a trainer? I don't believe it. You'll be bored in two days."

He shrugged. "Maybe, but I'll take boredom over this any day of the week. There was a time when I wouldn't have said that, but right now, I need a change. I have to do something different. I can't take chasing down criminals and interacting with the worst elements of society every single day for the rest of my life. It's too dark for me, too hopeless. I want something normal, even boring. That sounds good to me."

As he watched her walk away, he felt nothing but relief.

————

His small flat was located on a quiet street — even by Rockhampton standards. When he'd moved in there with his partner five years earlier, they'd been excited to be out of the action. They saw so much of that lifestyle at work that all they wanted when they came home was to find some peace away from the urban grind. But now that his partner was gone, it was so quiet, he couldn't bear it. He needed to be around people, but not drama. Was it possible? He wasn't sure, but he knew it was time for him to get out of town. To start fresh somewhere else. He'd always wanted to help people, but working for the force had become such a grind, he wasn't sure anything he did made a difference.

When he walked into the flat, he glanced around at the

piles of boxes stacked throughout the small living room. The moving truck was due to arrive at any moment. He only had time for a glass of water. The cake had been so sweet, it'd given him a sugar rush.

He strode to the kitchen, set his box of things down on the bench and found a glass. Then he filled it with water, downed it and set the glass back in the packing box. Just then he heard the sound of a truck backing into the driveway. He hurried to greet the movers and show them what they should take.

They were done in an hour, and he sent them off with a wave. Then he returned to his empty flat. It was even more depressing than it had been an hour ago. There were stains on the carpet where the couch had been. Cobwebs and dust in places he'd not seen since he moved in.

It was a fifteen-hour drive to Palm Beach where his new apartment was located, so he'd have to spend the night in Noosa, only six hours away. It wasn't lunchtime yet, so there was plenty of time to get the first leg of his trip done before nightfall.

His phone rang, and he pressed it to his ear. "Hello?"

"You still in Rocky, mate?" Brad's voice echoed down the line.

"Just leaving now."

"We'll miss you. Have a good trip."

"You're going to visit, right?" Callum asked.

Brad laughed. "Of course, mate. You'll be on the Gold Coast — surf, sand and beautiful women. Try to keep me away."

Callum chuckled along with him, but he knew the reality of Brad's life and career wouldn't give him much of a chance to make the long trip. He was a focused detective, one of the best on the force. Callum respected and liked him, probably better than anyone else. He hoped they could stay in touch, but he wasn't expecting much.

"I'll talk to you later, then," he said.

He hung up the phone and tucked it into his pocket. Then he sighed. "Goodbye and good riddance," he said out loud to the empty apartment.

Callum slung his rucksack onto his back and headed for the door. With one last backward glance over his shoulder, he pulled the door shut behind him, then marched to his truck. As he drove away, he turned up the radio, and a smile drifted across his face.

CHAPTER
Three

ONE WEEK LATER

I'm walking along the side of a road. No idea where I am. I'm lost. I feel it in the depths of my soul. No words to describe it, really—just a feeling. An ominous, aching thing like a ball or a rock in my chest. Looking down, I see my feet. They're small, bare. One of my toenails is chipped, and there's blood on the toe. It's wet and red, so it must've happened recently, although I don't feel a thing other than the gravel and pebbles beneath my soles, pushing up into my arches and making me wince.

I want to cry out for my mother, but I have no image in my mind of who she is or how she looks. I only know there's a guttural ache deep inside that wants out. And I'm reticent. I don't want to release it. If I do, what if I'm heard? Who knows what's out there? I'm alone. The only thing I see on both sides of the road, stretching into the distance either way, is bushland.

Dry trees, gums and bushes. Dry yellow stalks of grass in bunches clustered here and there as though they've been dropped in handfuls by a giant trundling through the countryside in a hurry.

"Mum!" I whisper it, but with force.

Still, I know there won't be a response.

My cheeks are wet with tears. I feel them oozing from my eyes, and I squeeze my eyelids shut.

Where is she? I can't say. But I know that she's abandoned me somehow. I'm too young to be angry. I'll forgive her anything at all if she'll just come and get me.

There's something on the road ahead. It seems like a stick at first, but as I stumble closer with my tiny, tiptoeing steps, it moves. It's long and slithers, black with sparkling eyes, in the direction of a road sign. The sign has something on it, but I can't read it. It's a red symbol with white around it. I know my colours, but not my numbers yet. Does that mean I'm two or maybe three years old? Surely by four I could recognise a numeral painted on a sign.

The question has me realising I'm dreaming, but that doesn't change the fact that I'm stuck here, in pain, waiting for a snake to get out of my path so I can keep hobbling down a road with no idea where I'm going. And I've been here before, in this very same dream, dozens of times, so I know it's not simply a dream, but a memory as well. Is it a true memory, or has it been tainted by the stories I've been told? There's no way for me to know, but in the moment, it doesn't matter because I'm here and it's very real and I know I must go on.

Somehow I know about snakes and not to touch it or go too close. Plus, I'm not as scared as I rationally think I should be. Then it's out of the way, and I'm moving forwards again. But the few moments standing still remind me just how hot the bitumen is beneath my feet. It's burning my soles until I wonder if it'll form blisters. But I can't move any faster, so I shuffle off to the side where there's dirt, gravel and a few patches of what looks to be dead grass.

I'm suddenly terribly aware of the air around me. It makes me cough. It's thick with smoke and growing thicker with each passing moment. I cough again, my eyes watering with the effort it takes to draw breath. I glance around, but I don't see any flames. Where's Mum? I need her. But I know she's not coming. I'm not sure how, but the realisation of it is embedded deep in my psyche. My father, too — I can't picture him, but I feel like he's missing from my life and I don't know why.

There's a noise on the road, and my head snaps in that direction, gaze fixed on the horizon where the road blurs into an orange sky. A car is coming. It's blue and long, like the neighbour's car — the one with the boot that opens up and you can crawl inside and lie down like it's a hard bed, and you can look out the long, rectangular windows on either side and see the clouds skipping across the blue sky.

The car pulls up nearby, tyres crackling in the gravel that lines the side of the road. There's a scared feeling buzzing in my stomach, and also, I'm hungry. So hungry that I feel nauseated. I just want to go home. But when I try to remember where that is, I only get scattered images — a blurred face, a smile, the scent of pikelets frying in a pan, and music on the radio.

A woman climbs out of the car and walks towards me. She's wearing a dress with birds on it. I like birds. They wake me up in the morning with their songs, and sometimes I sit on the patio and watch them duck and dive around the overgrown garden as the sun rises beyond the horizon, turning the dark sky to blue.

"Are you okay? Where's your mum?" the woman says.

I reach out my arms and whimper. It's all I can do. I can't seem to form words. And she looks kind, with wrinkles around the edges of a pair of large brown eyes.

"Oh, you poor little thing. Come with me. We've got to get out of here. The fire's coming."

———

Milly's eyes flew open, and she cried out. A quiet, insipid cry that sparked from the lump in her throat. It was a dream. Only a dream. She wasn't walking on the side of the road. She glanced down at the sheets tucked tightly around her prone body where it lay in the hard hospital bed. There was no smoke burning her lungs, no car and no woman with kind brown eyes.

The bed whirred slowly upwards, tilting Milly forwards. She shifted uncomfortably, wanting desperately to change position, but as she tried, she found she barely moved. Her lower body wasn't cooperating with her the way it usually did. She'd never fully appreciated until now how easy it was to think about moving and have her body respond immediately.

Milly set her mobile phone on the bedside table, a game still bright on the screen, and did her best to make herself comfortable, although she found movement difficult. Her thoughts were muddled from the painkillers, but she was beginning to get more and more clarity each day that passed. It'd been over a week since her accident — or so the nurse had told her first thing that morning when she was woken up to take her meds. But Milly couldn't recall much, if any, of that time. The entire week had been a blur of medical tests, bland food and changing faces. The accident was like a bad dream — images darted across her mind's eye when she was least expecting it, causing her breath to catch in her throat. But if she tried to picture the event and what happened after her fall, it only came to her in distant, muddy flickers, like a badly made claymation film.

A doctor stood at the foot of her bed, his round face turned towards the chart in his hands. "I'm Dr Lee. I'm here to give you an update on your prognosis. I've spoken with you before. Do you remember?"

She shook her head slowly. His face didn't look familiar. "No, sorry."

"That's okay," he crooned reassuringly. "It's normal for you to have some confusion after what you've been through. Very likely it will all come back to you. But for now, we'll simply keep going over the facts until they stick. Okay?"

She forced a smile. Her heart thudded against her ribcage.

It scared her that she couldn't remember seeing him before or listening as he talked through her prognosis. Did that mean her memory was gone as well as the feeling in her legs?

"Let's see how you're going, Amelia." He flicked through a few pages, then focused on her with a smile. "Looking good."

"Really?" Her heart stirred. Maybe things weren't as bad as she'd thought they were. They'd been running tests on her for days. Perhaps they'd discovered something she didn't know yet about her condition. Was there hope after all?

"Definitely. You've improved so much already. You've got good movement returning to your torso, arms and head, as you know. But I'm afraid your legs and feet seem to still be without both feeling and movement."

She sighed, her heart dropping. "Oh, I thought maybe you had news."

"If anything changes, you make sure to let me know. Okay?"

"Sure," she replied, her chin dropping.

"Do you have someone here with you?" he asked, glancing at the door to the shared hospital ward.

"My boyfriend is here somewhere, I think. I'm sure he'll be back in a minute."

"Let's wait for him, then," the doctor replied. A name badge on his white coat said he was a neurologist. Most often she was attended to by nurses, and they'd been an absolute godsend to her during what had been the most difficult and soul-crushing week of her entire life. She couldn't picture their faces, but she remembered their gentle touch, their soothing words, the way they had been there for her through the worst of her pain and the panic of being alone in the middle of the night with no idea where she was. It was a nurse who'd come to her, stroked her hair and calmed her sobbing. Nurse Dianna Northen was the only one she remembered. She'd been there that morning, taking care of

Milly with such gentle compassion it'd almost brought her to tears.

No matter what'd happened during her years as a foster child, she'd always had her own body to take refuge in — a body that'd been fit and strong and had carried her away from danger more times than she could count. Now that body was a crumpled mess, and she didn't know if it would ever be the same again.

Each day that passed without her regaining feeling in her legs brought her closer to the brink of despair.

Kevin stepped through the doorway and hesitated when he saw the doctor. His gaze travelled to Milly's face. "Am I interrupting?"

Dr Lee ushered him into the room. "No, no, come on in. We're about to have a discussion about Amelia's prognosis, and it's good that you're here with her."

Kevin walked to the bed and stopped beside Milly, crossing his arms over his chest.

Dr Lee set the chart back on the end of the bed and steepled his fingers together. "As I was just telling Amelia, all the testing we've done has shown no improvement in sensation or movement within her legs and feet. There has been substantial improvement everywhere else — recovery of both sensation and movement in her torso, arms and so on. But unfortunately, it hasn't been universal."

"Does that mean I won't ever walk again?" Milly asked as a stone formed deep inside.

The doctor paused. "Not necessarily. There's a lot of swelling. When that swelling goes down, we might see a return of some capability."

"But there's no guarantee?" Kevin asked.

Dr Lee shook his head. His thin hair shifted in place so it hung over his forehead. "No, I'm afraid not. It could mean paralysis for the rest of your life, and it's important that you face that prospect. I don't want to give you false hope because that would cause more psychological damage in the long term. You need to be prepared to adjust your lifestyle to adapt to your new needs. If in time you do find some sensation returning to your legs, that would be fantastic. But there's an equal chance that won't happen."

"So, fifty-fifty?" Milly asked. Her chest felt tight like something was squeezing the breath out of her. She couldn't accept what he was saying.

He nodded. "That's right. My estimation is that you have as good a chance of some level of healing as you do permanent paralysis. We just don't know."

When the doctor left, Kevin scrubbed both hands over his face with a groan. "This can't be happening."

He turned his back to her and strode to the window, staring out over the city of Brisbane. Skyscrapers were etched against the skyline, and birds flitted by the window. The sun set in the west, casting a gold-and-pink glow over the entire landscape. It was beautiful, but Milly couldn't appreciate it. She couldn't think of anything other than the doctor's words. What if she never walked again? How could she live that way?

"I'm so glad you're here," she whispered as a sob escaped her throat.

Kevin spun to face her, eyes wide. "Of course I had to be here. How would it look…?"

"What?"

"Listen." He walked back to the bed and took her hand in his. "I know you're probably feeling a bit upset about all of this right now, but I have to take a walk. I need some time to process what the doc said and to think about the future. I'll buy you some ice cream when I come back. Okay?"

She nodded. "Sure."

"See you in a bit."

He scurried from the room, and she watched him leave with a heavy heart. Could Kevin handle something like this?

Would he be there for her in the ways she needed? If she never walked again, he'd have to help her in and out of a wheelchair, probably bathe her and who knew what else. She'd never really thought about it before, but it was going to be challenging for both of them. For the first time in a long time, she was grateful to have him in her life. She shouldn't have taken him for granted all these years. Being alone was far worse than having someone, even if that person seemed like a mismatch at times.

She reached for the hairbrush on her bedside table and ran it through her long, thick hair. The brunette strands fell across her shoulder. It was awkward, trying to brush out the knots that'd formed over the past week without really being able to sit forward or balance using her legs. She tried raising her head, but her neck was still swollen and painful, and she let her head fall back against the pillow with a cry.

Tears formed in the corners of her eyes. Even the simplest things were so difficult now. Surely it wouldn't stay like this. It couldn't. She couldn't live this way. She was independent, young and strong. She had so much of life ahead of her. So many dreams of places to travel, adventures to undertake, things to do… Now she wouldn't be able to do any of them.

As tears fell down her cheeks, there was a knock at her door, Nurse Dianna, who'd taken care of her all week walked in.

"How are you feeling this afternoon, Milly?" she called in a steady voice as she bustled to the end of the bed to check the chart.

"Okay," Milly replied through a veil of tears.

Nurse Dianna looked up at her, compassion softening her features. "Oh, dear. What's happened then?"

"Dr Lee was just here and said I might not walk again."

Nurse Dianna stepped around the bed and rested against the side of it. She patted Milly's arm. "I'm sorry you have to face that. But you're strong enough to handle it. It's not the end of the world, or of your life."

"What do you mean? Of course it is!" Milly cried, her tears falling faster now.

The nurse shook her head slowly. "No, not by a long shot. Even if that happens, which is still very much an *if*, you can have a full and happy life. I know it might not seem like it, but we've had plenty of young people come through this ward, just like you. They thought their life was over when faced with their prognosis, but they've gone on to have full lives. It's not the way they thought it'd be—it's different to what they'd planned—but they're able to be happy, if they choose it."

"I'll never be happy again," Milly spat. "This is so unfair. Kevin can't even face it — he's gone for a walk and left me here to deal with all this alone."

"An injury like this will certainly test the mettle of everyone in your life. It's going to be hard on him as well. Give him some grace to work through it."

"I know…" Milly sighed. "I just wish he'd work through it *with* me."

"We're all different," Nurse Dianna replied. "And thank the Lord for that. Can you imagine if we were clones of each other? We'd drive one another to the brink." She chortled. "It's a good thing we're each unique—that's how we manage to get along so well. We've got different strengths and weaknesses, so when you're weak, Kevin can be strong, and when he's weak, you can step in for him. Do you see?"

Milly nodded. She understood the concept. She just wasn't sure it was true of her and Kevin. He never seemed to have the strength she needed, and she rarely felt the desire to step in to help him when he was going through something hard. Did that mean she was a bad person? Sometimes she wondered. He'd questioned whether she had a heart, and maybe she didn't. But whatever she had, it was aching now.

She'd always been called strong, resilient, a fighter by the people in her life. But she didn't feel strong now. She wasn't sure she could handle what was to come.

"What about your parents?" Nurse Dianna asked. "Whenever I ask you about them, you seem to clam up. Can I call them for you? I haven't seen them here all week. Do they know what's happened?"

Milly wiped her cheeks dry with a tissue from her nightstand. "I don't have parents."

Nurse Dianna frowned. "Who raised you?"

"I was a foster kid." Milly blew her nose.

"Have you stayed in touch with any of your foster parents?"

She sighed. There was only one woman she'd kept contact with. "My last foster mother, Hannah Bigsby. Although I haven't spoken to her in months."

"Let's call her," Nurse Dianna suggested.

"I don't know…"

"I'm sure she'd want to know what's happened."

Milly wasn't so certain. She'd been a difficult teenager and had hardly spoken to the woman she affectionately called "Mama" since she moved out. Whenever she missed the idea of family — when she saw someone else surrounded by it, or when she watched a movie that glamorised it—it was an image of Hannah's lined face, smiling broadly at some joke that one of the foster kids made, that flitted through her thoughts.

Hannah always said that Milly was so funny, something no one else had ever accused her of before or since. Hannah loved to laugh, and she'd laughed all the time. A great big belly laugh that shook her whole body and spread to anyone else in the room. She'd been the only foster mother who'd made Milly feel safe and loved. If she wanted anyone by her side at this time, it was Hannah. But would Hannah want to be there?

CHAPTER

Four

IT WASN'T until the next day that Milly finally built up the courage to call Hannah. Kevin hadn't left his hotel room yet, hadn't checked in with her and was probably still sound asleep. There were no nurses around. Milly had a few minutes alone to think, and the only thing she could think of was hearing Hannah's voice again. The memories that had trickled into her mind over the past few days had now become a torrent of images, feelings and reminders of those brief few years living under Hannah's roof along with an assembly line of foster sisters.

She tucked her brown locks behind her ears and reached for her mobile phone. It'd charged all night, so it had plenty of battery left. But no one had called her in days anyway, so it'd hardly mattered. Kevin texted whenever he had anything to say. The first few days in the hospital, he'd been with her in her room for hours, but in more recent days, that time had shrunk to a half an hour here or there throughout the day. She'd tried to speak to him more than once about what he was thinking or feeling since the doctor announced the previous day that she might never walk again, but he'd refused to engage with her. Maybe he'd be able to face up to a conversation today. They had to speak sometime. He would be her support person—there were things to work out.

With one last exhale, she dialled the number. She'd saved it years ago in her contacts list and hoped Hannah hadn't changed the number.

"Hello?"

"Hi, Mama. It's Milly." She steadied her voice. "Sorry I haven't called…"

"Never mind all that. It's so good to hear from you. Where are you? What's going on?" There was concern in Hannah's voice.

"I've had an accident."

By the time Milly had explained everything to Hannah, she was crying silent tears. She didn't want her foster mother to know how upset she was, but she couldn't stop the tears from wetting her cheeks.

"I'm still living in Palm Beach, so I'll be there in about an hour," Hannah said.

"You don't have to come," Milly explained. "I thought you might like to know, but I don't expect anything."

"Of course I'm coming. I'm slow-moving these days, but I'll be there. Don't you worry about that, sweetheart."

———

Half an hour later, Kevin finally showed. His hair was still wet, and he had sheet marks on the side of his face. He hadn't shaved in days, and dark stubble covered his chin and cheeks. He yawned before kissing her. "Sorry, I slept in. I'm exhausted. This has been a tough week."

"No worries," Milly replied. "It's been tough for both of us. I'm glad you got some rest."

He sat on the chair beside her bed. The ward was busy, with most of the beds full. The nearby lifts ran incessantly, opening their doors with a ding every minute or so. There were doctors, physiotherapists, morning tea deliveries and more. The place was a madhouse; it was impossible to get any rest. Milly couldn't wait until she was able to leave but had no idea when that might be.

"I called Hannah, my foster mother," she said suddenly.

His eyes widened. "Really? Why?"

"I thought she'd like to know what's going on."

"But you don't ever talk to her… It's not like you're close."

"I know…" How could she explain to someone like Kevin who saw everything in black and white? He spoke to his parents daily. They were his yardstick for judging a healthy familial relationship, but that's just not how Milly operated. Her connections were more complicated than that. She loved Hannah fiercely, yet at the same time kept her at arm's length. She couldn't explain it any more than she could explain why she avoided taking her relationship with Kevin to the next level. It made no sense—it was simply the way she was.

"Is she coming to see you?"

"Yes, but it will take her a while to get here. She lives in Palm Beach, and she's getting older. She was already in her sixties when she fostered me. She'd been doing it most of her life, and I was one of the last kids she took in. There were seven other girls who came and went at the time I was there — my foster sisters. But after I graduated and left, she stopped fostering and closed down the cafe that she'd run for years."

"Wow, you broke her, huh?" He grinned and rubbed his stubbled chin.

She huffed. "I prefer to believe I was irreplaceable."

"Sure," he said with a sarcastic drawl. "That must've been it."

"Anyway, she'll probably arrive soon. I thought maybe you could get some coffee for us from across the street and give us a chance to talk?"

He sighed. "That sounds nice, and I'd be happy to do it, but there's something we need to discuss."

"Oh?" She reached for the water bottle by the bed and took a sip. She was still attached to a drip, but Nurse Dianna had encouraged her to get back into drinking and eating normally so she could find a new life rhythm as soon as possible.

"You don't want to be in this place forever, do you?" the nurse had asked as she'd fixed the crumpled sheets over Milly's unfeeling legs.

"Definitely not," Milly had replied, although she wasn't sure how she could ever leave without walking. How would she live? What would she do without the staff here to help her with it all? Dread and despondency settled over her shoulders like a cape.

Kevin was talking, and she'd missed some of what he'd said. She'd been doing that lately — drifting in and out of conversations. It was almost as though she'd hit the mute button on the television remote. His lips were moving, but his words didn't reach her conscious thoughts.

"Sorry. What did you say?" she asked.

His brow furrowed, and he tapped the ends of his fingers on the bedside table as he settled back in the armchair. "Are you listening?"

"Yes, of course." She blinked.

"I've got to get back to Longreach. I'm needed at work, and I've got that family barbecue this weekend. Mum wants me to pick up the drinks on my way there. No one else can do it. They're all busy."

"You're leaving me here so you can pick up drinks on the way to a barbecue?" Was she hearing him correctly? Surely he didn't mean it. She wasn't ready to be alone yet. She couldn't do anything herself. Couldn't even reach her phone if it was a centimetre too far from her grasp.

"You've got a whole team here caring for you. There's

nothing much for me to do." His face reddened. "I'd stay, but..."

"But what?"

"You don't really need me. Do you?"

"Of course I do. I'm completely alone."

"Your foster mother is coming today. You've got nurses in and out of here every five minutes. You're not alone." He shook his head, unable to meet her gaze.

"I can't believe it..." She didn't finish the sentence. Instead, she stared at her hands, clasped over the blanket across her lap. Five years of her life with a man who didn't care enough to stay for more than a week when she was going through the worst.

"You know I'm not good with this kind of stuff." He waved a hand in her direction.

"What kind of stuff is that, Kev?"

"Sickness and things like that. I don't like hospitals. I'm not the person you call if you're throwing up or have a fever. It's just not something I've ever been good at."

"No one likes hospitals, Kev. But you suck it up for the person you love. You deal with it like an adult."

"Don't talk to me about being an adult, Milly," he spat, his tone changing to one filled with bitterness. "You're the one who didn't want the commitment. Well, now I'm calling it. We're not a committed couple, and I can't do this. I'm going home."

He stood to his feet, still not looking at her. Instead, his gaze flitted to the doorway and back to his feet as though seeking escape.

Her head was muddy. Her mind seemed not quite attached to her body, like she was floating slightly outside of herself. She heard her own voice, but it sounded strange.

"I guess you should leave, then."

He studied her for a moment, then turned on his heel. At

the doorway, he glanced back. "You were never going to be what I needed." And then he was gone.

She contemplated his words. What he needed? What about what *she* needed?

Pain radiated through her, but her eyes were dry. She rarely cried, and she wondered again if she was emotionally broken in a way that could never be fixed, like her body. But the only thing she felt now that Kevin was gone was a slight sense of relief mixed with anger and a rising panic about what she'd do. One thing she'd learned in life was that it was only a matter of time until the people you love left you. She'd loved her parents—at least, she thought she must've done. But they'd abandoned her on the side of the road when she was three years old. Every foster parent, other than Hannah, had pushed her on to the next family.

She must've drifted off to sleep because when she woke next, the foggy feeling in her head was gone and the pain in her neck and back had seeped in like the rising tide — a tide that drove her up into the soft sand dunes on Palm Beach to walk amongst the seagrass and crab holes. She grimaced and attempted to scoot into a more comfortable position, but the twinge of pain that came elicited a yelp and she quickly stopped moving.

"What's wrong?" asked a voice.

She turned her head to see Hannah rising to her feet from the worn armchair beside her. "Mama!"

Emotion threatened to overwhelm her as Hannah shuffled to the bed and bent to kiss her forehead. "My darling girl. I didn't want to wake you. You seemed to be having a nice, deep slumber."

Milly reached up and encircled Hannah's neck, and the two of them embraced awkwardly. It was difficult for Milly to do anything at all, but hugging was especially cumbersome.

"Thanks for coming," she said as a lump rose into her throat.

"Are you on your own here?" Hannah asked.

Milly inhaled a sharp breath. "I'm afraid so. Kevin was here, my boyfriend. But he left."

"I'm sorry. Is he coming back?"

"I don't think so." Saying the words made it even more real. It hadn't been a dream, and surprisingly Milly had remembered every painful moment of their earlier conversation. At least that was something—her brain wasn't quite so unreliable as it had been.

Hannah pulled the chair closer to sit and took her hand. She'd aged in the years since Milly had seen her last. She carried herself with a stoop, looked thinner than ever, and her hair was now entirely grey and worn in a small bun at the top of her head, with wisps and tendrils hanging down around her neck and face.

"It's good to see you." Milly squeezed her hand.

"And you, dear girl. I get your messages every now and then. I love keeping up with what you're doing. You've become quite the horsewoman, it seems."

Milly's stomach clenched. "Not good enough, I'm afraid."

"Accidents happen to all of us. No one is perfect. But you'll bounce back from this."

"The doctor says I might not walk again."

Hannah sighed. "I'm sorry to hear that."

"I don't know what I'll do."

"One thing I know is that you'll work it out. Just like you always do. It might seem impossible to face the future right now, but one day at a time and you'll find a way."

"It *is* impossible."

"Nothing is impossible with God on your side."

Milly held back a snarky reply. She'd never shared Hannah's faith, but she respected that the woman stuck to it no matter what came. Whatever Hannah had endured in life seemed to have strengthened her faith rather than diminished it. Every Sunday, she attended a small timber chapel for a service, and every morning, she spent time on her knees on the back veranda with a large-print Bible at her side. It was one of the few things Milly had learned to rely on when she lived with Hannah — she could find her on the veranda first thing, and Hannah would always have a smile and kind word for her.

"Thanks, Hannah. I know you're just trying to encourage me, but I'm not sure I can be encouraged. I'm feeling pretty hopeless. I didn't go to university, I didn't get a profession—I wanted to be a horse trainer. And now look at me. I have no skills, no prospects, and if I can't walk, I definitely can't train. How will I pay the bills?" The lump in her throat felt as though it might choke her.

"We'll figure it out."

She'd never been part of a family other than those few years with Hannah and her foster sisters. Before that, and since, she'd been completely alone in the world. Even with Kevin and his family, she'd never been fully accepted. Not one of the group. But having Hannah here with her had opened something up inside of her — emotions swirled beneath the surface. She couldn't let them out, couldn't let go of the control she'd kept over herself for so many years, but she felt them working to break free deep down inside her.

It would be such a relief to simply let go. To cry, or wail, or shout about how unfair her life had been. But she wasn't going to do that because it wouldn't change anything. As the emotions drained away, she felt nothing but hopelessness — powerless to change anything, unable to fix what was broken and unsure of how she could face the future.

CHAPTER

Five

CALLUM TOSSED AND TURNED, sweat coating his body. He cried out as if in pain, then his eyes flew open and he blinked away the sleep. He'd been dreaming again. The dream was never the same, but it always followed the same theme. Darkness, violence, loss. The pain of loss had formed a lump in his throat as he slept. Shame washed over him, and he rolled into a sitting position, cradling his head in both hands. How could he ever move on and get the past out of his head if it invaded his very dreams? He'd managed to push his feelings aside during waking hours, but he seemed to have no control over his thought life while he was slumbering.

Outside the studio apartment, the waves shushed against the shoreline. He'd thought the ocean would bring nighttime relief with its steady rhythmic comfort, but it hadn't seemed to make any inroads into his nightmares. They'd given him a break for the first few weeks, when he'd fallen into his bed in utter exhaustion after the move and the renovations he'd thrown himself into immediately upon arrival. But now that he'd been living in Palm Beach for three months, they were back with a vengeance. Maybe he should train harder, make himself more tired. It was worth a try.

He quickly changed into some running gear and a hat and headed out the back door, down the long, narrow flight of timber steps, and then leapt over the short hedgerow beside the backyard he shared with the other small apartment block residents. Beside the hedge was a worn pathway in the sand that meandered through the brush and dunes to the beach. He ran the entire path, dodging around a trio of surfers who were jogging in the same direction with surfboards beneath an arm and wetsuits half-zipped.

"Hey, slow down, mate!" one of them called after him.

But he paid no mind. He didn't intend to slow down. Not now, and maybe not ever. Not while the demons of the past continued to chase him. He ran at full speed down the beach to the waterline where the sand was moist and hard-packed. He always got sand in his joggers, but he didn't like to run barefooted, so he put up with it.

Living at the beach was a new thing for him, but he'd always wanted to. The responsible man he'd been hadn't taken the plunge. There were things to do, tasks to complete, responsibilities to manage. Selling up and moving to the coast would be a luxury, and he didn't have time or money for luxuries. He was a public servant, a man of the people. His responsibilities to his parents kept him in Rockhampton at first, but then they'd moved. By that time, he was engaged to Beth Monaghan and working for the force. And so he stayed.

Now, he was no longer a police officer, and Beth had broken his heart. One day, while working out, when he'd considered the multitude of ways his life had fallen apart, he realised that he no longer had any obligation to anyone. That his ambitions for promotion had been achieved — he was a detective, and it hadn't turned out to be the fulfilling career he'd hoped and dreamed it would be. He could leave any time he chose. So, he started planning. And it'd taken him a year to make the move.

After half an hour, he reached the end of several beaches joined by rocky outcroppings that he hopped across before continuing. The sky overhead was brilliantly blue now that the sun had risen completely, and the heat had already intensified so that the sweat poured down his forehead and into his eyes. The hat kept some of it at bay, but for the rest, he had to swipe repeatedly with his hand to keep from being blinded.

Then he turned around and ran back home again. Seagulls leapt out of his way, squawking. He sprayed wet sand and salt water up the back of his legs when he ran through the rising tide, and finally he was home again. It'd taken him a few weeks to recognise the various houses, apartment buildings and neighbours along his route, but now he knew them all by heart.

He wondered what Beth was doing now that he was gone. No doubt she'd already moved on and hadn't given him a second thought. Brad was another matter. After everything that'd happened, he'd done his best to keep his friendship with Brad strong, but it was difficult to stay open while keeping so much hidden at the same time, and they didn't have the same closeness they'd had once upon a time. But that could also have been due to the fact that Callum wasn't the same person he'd been then. None of them were.

Back at the apartment, he showered and dressed in smart-casual shorts and a collared T-shirt, along with joggers and his favourite cross necklace. The drive to his new office was only ten minutes away, and when he got there, he couldn't help smiling. His office was attached to a gym. There were six of them affiliated with the gymnasium as personal trainers. He had a specialisation in injury recovery, which he'd studied through a university online. He'd relished the challenge of the courses at the time but now was grateful he'd made the effort as it'd given him an entirely new career, and one that he was already enjoying.

"Good morning, Brenda," he said to the woman behind the reception counter.

Brenda Zurl nodded, her brown curls bouncing, and waved as she chattered to someone on the telephone headset she wore constantly.

"You're early today," his boss said from the glass-walled office where he sat behind a large oak desk.

Callum sat at his desk in the open office space, setting his small backpack on the floor by his feet. "I couldn't sleep. It's getting hot in the mornings."

"You should invest in an air conditioner."

"It's nowhere near as bad as Rocky," Callum countered with a grin. "You're just soft."

"Trust me, you'll get as soft as me in no time. Anyway, why torture yourself?"

"You're right—life is short. I'll look into it. But for now, I've got to remember to turn on the fan at night because I'm waking up in a pile of sweat."

"Happy thought," Ted replied with a grimace as he brushed back his black hair with long, tanned fingers. "Thanks for that visual. Hey, come in and shut the door for a minute. I've got a new client in the pipeline I think would be a perfect fit for you."

———

When Milly opened her eyes the next morning, Hannah was there again, knitting needles clinking. A cloth bag lay open at her feet, and a thread of thick, purple wool pulled taut, then released and went taut again as she knitted. She wore a pair of glasses perched on the end of her nose and peered over them when Milly yawned.

"You're awake. They've got you on some strong painkillers, I'd imagine."

Milly smiled. "It helps, although the pain doesn't seem to be as bad as it was when I first arrived."

"Maybe you should wean yourself a little then, honey. These places will get you hooked faster than you can say opiates."

"Really? Don't the doctors know best?" she asked.

Hannah set down her knitting on top of the bag and rose to her feet with a grunt. "The doctors are amazing, and they're doing the best they can, but some of these pills are a little much. And they're addictive. You remember what I always used to tell you?"

Milly pursed her lips. How could she forget? "You have to take care of yourself. You can't count on anyone else to do it."

"That's right. Even when it comes to your health. You're the one who knows your own body and how you feel, and you've got to trust your own instincts. And you've got to be careful how you treat this body of yours. You've only got one."

Milly's heart fell. She only had one body, and she'd done so much damage to it, she might never recover. What if she never walked again?

It was the same thing every morning, now that she was more aware of what was going on — when she woke, she'd feel good and have hope. Then the realisation of her situation would dawn all over again. The plummeting feeling inside sent her into a brief panic spiral before she gathered control over her emotions and pushed them down, deep down, covering them with apathy all over again.

"I can't do this," she whispered as the panic subsided. "It's too hard."

Hannah took her hand. "I'm sorry, love. Was that my fault? I shouldn't have said anything."

"No, it's not you. It's waking up — I remember what

happened and what I'll live with for the rest of my days. It's like experiencing it again. Hearing the doctor's words for the first time. I hope it won't be this way forever."

Hannah patted her arm. "Of course it won't, my love. You've just been through a trauma, and your mind is trying its best to cope. You're young and healthy, so you have a lot going for you. I don't think it's time to throw your hands in the air just yet."

"Even if I could…" Milly scoffed. "It hurts too much."

Hannah offered a wry smile. "Yes, even if you could. You know, you've always been strong."

"I don't know about that," Milly replied. "I don't feel strong most of the time."

"But you are. You've been through hard situations before, and you made it."

"Worse than this?"

"I don't think you can compare. I know your boyfriend's left you here, and you've got injuries that may last a long time, perhaps forever. But when your parents abandoned you — that was hard too. I didn't find you until you were almost grown, but I remember how tough you were. Nothing fazed you. I couldn't get you to show any kind of emotion for the longest time. You held it all in, and you were in control. You didn't let people get you down, and you wouldn't take a compliment, either."

"Some people would say those aren't great traits," Milly replied with a sigh. "I'd like to think I've improved a little since then."

"I didn't see it that way at all. You'd been through so much, and you didn't let it get to you. You held your chin high and powered through. If you had to protect yourself while you did it, well, who can blame you for that?"

"I wish there was someone I could ask about my early years. I don't remember anything at all. I've been told they found me on the side of the road when I was about three years old, but I can't recall what happened. I don't know who my parents were. I don't know anything about myself, really. Did they tell you anything about me?"

She studied Hannah's face, anxious for some kind of reaction. Even when they'd lived together, Hannah had been tight-lipped about Milly's past. Either she didn't know anything, or she believed Milly would be better off not knowing. If it was the latter, Milly was an adult now. She deserved the truth even if knowing it was painful.

Hannah sat back in the chair and picked up her knitting. "I don't know much more than you, I'm afraid. You were found by some people driving by, I believe. Such a shame. Whoever was caring for you sure did let you down, and you didn't deserve that." Her cheeks grew redder as she spoke. "I'm sorry, love. I wish I could've been there for you, but I didn't know."

"That's okay. Like I said, I don't recall any of it. And I guess it made me stronger."

"I pray that you'll find happiness someday. You've been through enough of the hard stuff—it's time for some good to come your way," Hannah muttered, her knitting speed increasing.

"Thanks, Mama. But I don't think it's in the cards for me. I'm not that lucky." Milly stared down at her unmoving legs.

Hannah set down her knitting again, her eyes bright. "Luck has nothing to do with it, my love."

"Whether it's luck or something else entirely, I'm afraid I missed out when it was being divvied up."

Hannah chortled. "We'll just see about that." She grimaced and clutched at her heart.

"What is it? What's wrong?" Milly asked. She'd been alarmed at how elderly Hannah looked when she first walked into the hospital ward, but she'd been so preoccupied with what she was going through, she hadn't thought of it again.

"Oh, nothing. Some heartburn, no doubt. I'm getting older, my love. And it's not as much fun as you might think."

"Isn't it nice not to have all those foster kids running around your house anymore? You must be enjoying the peace and quiet."

Hannah laughed. "Oh, it wasn't so bad. I loved the noise and the clutter. It made me feel young to have you all racing around the house. Now it's so quiet, it feels like a morgue." She crossed her eyes and poked out her tongue.

Milly had forgotten how silly Hannah could be at times. It was one of the things she'd always loved about the older woman. "So, it wasn't all bad? Sometimes I feel as though I was more trouble than you really signed up for."

"You?" Hannah huffed. "Not a chance. You were wonderful. You had attitude, and sometimes you let it rule your tongue, but I didn't worry about you too much. Now your sister Emily—that was another story. She was trouble every day of the week. My, oh my, how many wrinkles she gave me."

A memory of her foster sister's impish face and chestnut ponytail flashed through Milly's mind. Her heart ached at the realisation that she hadn't seen Emily in over five years. Why was she so good at putting people out of her thoughts and setting them aside so she could go on with her life?

"What's Emily doing these days?" she asked.

An orderly came in with her breakfast tray, pushing the table into place so it was above Milly's lap. "There you go," he said with a smile. "Just let me know if you need anything else."

"Okay, thanks," Milly replied, reaching for the juice cup to open it.

She sipped while Hannah spoke. "She's singing here and there. Doing pretty well, too, from what she's told me. She's got a few regular gigs."

"She has such an amazing voice. I'm glad for her. It's a hard industry to break into, so she's clearly put in the work."

"From memory, she has a band, I believe. And they've been gigging together for a few years now. She was studying at the Queensland Conservatorium of Music, but I'm not sure if she's still there. I haven't spoken to her in a few months. She's pretty good about staying in touch, but sometimes she'll go for half a year before I hear from her again. Of course, I was only her parent for five years. She had several others before me."

"It seems like all the teen girls no one else wanted ended up at your door." Milly took a bite of toast with Vegemite. She loved to slather it with a thick layer of butter while it was still hot, but the toast at the hospital was always cold before it got to her. Still, as hungry as she was, it tasted good. At least her appetite was returning. That had to be a good sign.

"I asked for it. It's what I loved to do. I wish I could keep doing it, but of course, I'm getting on in years and it's a bit hard for me. When you and Emily left, I was ready to give it up. I wasn't sure I had room in my heart for any more girls. And I was tired." She laughed. "I retired after you left, I didn't have it in me anymore."

"I know it must've been difficult to give up the café."

"I hated to do it, but it was too much to be on my feet all day every day like that. Still, I love to cook, as you know. So, now I cook meals for refugee families and people who are displaced by the floods or homelessness. That kind of thing. Gives me a chance to help without wearing me out too much."

Milly had always been perplexed by how much of herself Hannah gave to the people around her. She'd never married or had children of her own. Instead, she'd spent her life serving those who needed it in whatever way she could, even to the point of wearing herself out, sacrificing her health, her vacation time, her money and everything she had to help others. And Milly had been one of them.

"Thanks for everything you do, Mama. You're amazing. I'm so grateful for you, and I know I haven't said that enough. I'm sorry I didn't stay in touch. I find it hard to express my feelings, but I hope you know how I feel about you." She sniffled.

Hannah stood and shuffled over to the bed. She bent over to embrace Milly. "It's okay, honey. I know how you feel, though it's nice to hear it. And I feel the same way."

CHAPTER
Six

BY THAT AFTERNOON, Milly was alone again and feeling particularly despondent. Hannah had tried to cheer her up, but the doctor visited again and didn't have any further news for her. She'd asked if she could reduce her pain relief, and he'd agreed, so her mind was clearer and her thoughts more pragmatic. If she couldn't walk, she couldn't work, which meant she wouldn't be able to pay her rent, and she'd lose her flat. What would happen to all her things? She could hardly drive out to Longreach and load them into a moving van on her own. And even if she could, where would she take them?

She had to face facts. As soon as they released her from the hospital, she was on her own and had nowhere to go. She could ask Hannah to take her back, but that wasn't fair since she was clearly fragile, and despite what she'd said, Milly could tell something was wrong with her health. She'd lost weight and shuffled rather than walked wherever she went. And she'd been pale in the face when she pressed a hand to her heart, even in the midst of her denials.

Milly had talked herself into such a state of despair that by the time someone tapped on the wall beside her bed to announce their arrival, she was ready to snap their head off if they poked it through her privacy curtain.

"Come in," she said in a glum voice.

A man peered around the curtain. He looked to be in his mid-thirties and had a handsome face. His hair was neatly combed to one side, and he wore a collared blue T-shirt that accentuated his biceps. He was clearly a jock and not her type at all, not that anyone was her type today. She would've snarled at a puppy with the way she felt. And he was no puppy.

"Hi, I'm your new personal trainer. I've been assigned to help you with the physiotherapy program your therapist put in place?"

"Is that a question?"

He looked at the clipboard in his hand and back at her again. "Amelia Wilson?"

"That's me," she replied. "And if my physiotherapist spoke to you, I'm sure she would've relayed that she's tried to run through the program with me but I'm just not ready. I can't do any of the things she wants me to do. My back still hurts, and I'm on painkillers. So, if you can come back some other day, that would be great."

She wanted to roll onto her side away from him and pretend the world didn't exist, but it was too difficult, and anyway, it was one of the many things she still couldn't do since the accident almost a month earlier.

"She did tell me you've been having some trouble adjusting." He settled himself beside her bed without asking and put the clipboard down on top of the covers. She wanted to shout at him that he could shove his clipboard someplace dark, but resisted the urge.

"I'm not having trouble adjusting. I've adjusted completely. I'm never going to walk again, and I've come to terms with that. Why should I try to do therapy exercises I can't manage? All it does is make me even more angry than I already am, and it exhausts me."

"Why does it bother you to be exhausted? That can be a good thing," he said, his eyes sparkling as his perfect set of white teeth flashed at her. "It means you've worked hard, and that's something to be proud of."

He was too much. Too perky, too positive, too handsome and too muscular. Why would the physio have sent her someone like this glass-half-full, athletic, attractive man to do therapy with her when she had to know all it would do would make Milly want to bury herself in a hole and never climb out again? He reminded her of all the things she'd never have in her life, all the things she'd lost. The beauty, the strength and adventure. She wouldn't fall in love, or have a first kiss again, or find someone to share her life with, or run, or climb, or lift weights. It was all in her past, and she hadn't done enough of any of it in her twenty-six years. She'd taken so many things for granted and assumed she'd still get to do them one day. If only she could go back in time and do everything differently, but she couldn't.

"I can see you're working some things through, and that's okay. But we're going to get started while you think about it."

His chipper voice grated down her spine, and she considered whacking him with the breakfast tray. If only she hadn't finished her juice—she would've enjoyed watching it stain his light-blue top. It wasn't like her to be so angry, but it felt good. She almost laughed at the pleasure she got in letting embracing her feelings. Normally she shoved them down as hard as she could, hiding them away in the dark recesses of her mind. But now she was releasing them, and she revelled in it.

"I don't want to. I've already told you that. I've injured my back, and I will never walk again. There's no point in trying to rehabilitate me—I'm beyond rehabilitation. So, off you go, back to your perky little life with your perfect wife and two-point-five children. You can forget all about me, and I'll certainly forget about you."

He blinked, then his eyes narrowed. "I don't have a wife or children, but thanks for the reminder."

She huffed. "Well…" She didn't know what to say to that. Had she hurt his feelings? Because she was just getting started, and it was disappointing to believe she'd already drawn blood. It wasn't as fun as she'd thought it might be.

He reached for her hand and began moving her arm up and down, straightening her fingers, pushing them back, stretching out the muscles. Every movement hurt a little bit, but not as much as she'd thought it would. His touch was gentle, and before long, it soothed her until she relaxed and the pain subsided.

"It's much easier when you don't fight me," he said.

She bit down on her lip. What else could she do? She couldn't walk away. He was in charge, in control of her life at that moment, and she hated it. Hated being out of control, having someone else in charge. Hated relying on anyone for help. The nurses were different. She'd formed relationships with them, needed them when she was at her worst. But she was feeling better, stronger, and he'd come in to push her around without asking first. Still, there was nothing she could do about it, so she'd put up with it for now. But as soon as he left, she'd have words with her doctor about him.

"There's not really anything I can do about it, is there?"

He laughed. "I guess not. You're stuck with me."

"You didn't even tell me your name."

"Oh, yeah. I was busy being yelled at." He winked at her, and she bit back a retort. "I'm Callum. It's nice to meet you, Amelia."

"Milly," she replied. "No one calls me Amelia."

"Milly it is, then." He moved to the other arm. "I'm going to come to see you daily while you're still in the hospital. Then when you transition to the rehab centre, I'll join you there in the gym. They have a fantastic facility, and you'll be strong again in no time."

She sighed. The rehab facility — she was dreading it. She wouldn't have Nurse Dianna to watch over her any longer. The doctors wouldn't be around. What if something went wrong? And what happened next? She couldn't stay in rehab forever. Just the thought of moving brought panic into her chest, making her head light.

"Everything okay?" Callum asked, concern etched on his handsome face. His cheeks were chiselled and his hair was short, as if he'd served in the military. His whole demeanour was disciplined and contained.

"Fine," she replied. "Did you serve in the military?"

He cocked his head to one side as he moved her covers out of the way and began stretching one of her legs. "How did you work that out?"

"You look like a digger. You've got that demeanour."

"Oh? It's the hair, isn't it?"

"That and the way you stand."

"Well, you're right. I was in the military for four years and then the police force after that."

"Huh. That explains it." She smirked.

"Explains what?"

"Oh, nothing. Why did you leave?"

"I was ready for something else. What about you? What do you do?"

"*Did.* You should get used to using the past tense. I used to be a horse trainer. Now… I have no idea what I'll do. Probably starve to death on the streets." She offered a hollow laugh. It was the truth — she didn't have a plan. And in her experience, people without a plan ended up with nothing.

"You won't starve to death on the streets unless you decide that's all you're good for."

"What does that mean?" she snipped, anger rising and burning in her cheeks.

"I mean that you're going to have to make some choices about your future. What you're going to do, how you're going to think, what you'll believe. Those are all choices."

"I don't have a choice about whether I'll walk again. And if a horse trainer can't walk, she can't train a horse. It's pretty simple. Plus, since I'm not a trust fund baby, if I don't train, I can't pay for rent or food."

She had no one. There wasn't a single person in the world, besides Hannah, who cared whether she hung around. And at the moment, she wasn't sure she cared enough about herself to keep going either. A lump filled her throat, and she ducked her head to keep him from seeing the glimmer of tears in her eyes. She wasn't a crier, but now she had no reason to hold back.

Even Kevin, the one person who was supposed to love her more than anyone else, had walked out on her the moment it got too hard. She'd tried calling him a few times to see if he'd made it home, but he hadn't returned her calls. He was gone, and she'd bet good money he wasn't coming back.

Callum didn't answer. He simply kept stretching out her legs and then helped her into a sitting position and swung her legs down over the side of the bed. She thought she would fall, and her hands flew out involuntarily to clutch at his shirt.

He gently helped her to lie on her back again and then rolled her onto her side.

She cleared her throat. "What is all this?"

"I'm working out what you can do and can't do. Does any of that hurt? Your doctor said you're able to sit and roll over, so that's what we're working on. It's amazing how quickly you're improving, given what I saw on your chart. But that's the benefit of being young and healthy."

"No, it doesn't hurt." It surprised her, actually. She'd thought for sure she'd be in extreme pain with the movements he was doing. There was a dull ache where the bruising remained, but otherwise, she felt good.

"You're doing really well. Just a few more exercises, and we'll be done for the day. I'll come up with a plan for your recovery, and we can work on it tomorrow. Is your husband around?" His brown eyes were earnest and full of compassion.

She looked away, staring at a blank space of wall to keep her emotions in check. "I'm not married, and my boyfriend walked out when the doctor told him my legs were officially useless. Does that count?"

She turned her angry glare on him and found herself wanting to scream or hit something. It wasn't fair. None of it was fair. Her entire life, she'd done everything she could to move beyond the tragedies of her early years, and for a while, she'd thought she might have managed it. She had a good job, a cute boyfriend, a boss who didn't despise her. Things were better than they'd been in a long time. But all that was gone now in one single flash of stupidity. She should've known better than to get on that horse. She *did* know better. She'd been reluctant to do it, but she wanted to prove herself. And now she'd pay for that pride for the rest of her life.

"He left you?" A muscle in Callum's jaw tightened.

"Yep. He's not coming back, and you can spare me the pity. I'm used to it. It's nothing new. And anyway, I did this, so maybe I deserve it." She fixed her attention on the muted television set that hung from the opposite wall. If she could keep herself distracted, the emotional tsunami that swelled beneath the surface would dissipate and she could go back to being her normal, sarcastic, glass-half-empty, apathetic self.

"You didn't do this. It was an accident." Callum's voice was so soft, she almost couldn't hear him.

He finished working on her feet with a few minutes of massage. "You really shouldn't have waited so long to start your therapy, you know. It's set you back a bit."

"What does it matter?" she spat.

He inhaled a slow breath, his gaze fixed on hers. "You can dial back the attitude a little. I'm on your side, you know?"

She huffed. "Whatever. You might as well just give up on me. Everyone else has."

"I'm sorry to hear that." He crossed his arms over his chest. "But that's the one thing I'm not going to do."

His words took her by surprise, and she turned her attention to him. He studied her with a curiosity and compassion that made her breath catch in her throat.

"Well…"

"I don't follow the rules—you should know that. But I promise to do my best. And between us, we'll get you into the best shape we can, if you'll trust me."

She didn't get a chance to respond. He turned on his heel and left the room, tapping his forehead as though he was in the military as he ducked through the door.

"Argh!" she moaned as soon as he was out of sight. He was so frustrating. All she wanted to do was lie in bed without being disturbed. Instead, she had some former military, muscle-bound trainer wanting to whip her into shape. For what purpose? She couldn't bear the thought of him watching her fail, the look of disappointment as he walked away from her and gave up — just like she knew he would. As much as she'd tried to shake off that legacy, it'd followed her and entrapped her all over again, and now she knew she'd never be free of it.

CHAPTER

Seven

TWO MONTHS to the day after she'd first arrived in the hospital, Amelia was transferred to the outpatient facility for rehabilitation. It wasn't far from the hospital campus, only about a ten-minute drive, and they'd organised a wheelchair and a van to take her there. The entire process was fairly straightforward, although she was sad to be leaving.

Panic rose up like bile in her throat when she turned around in her chair one last time to look at the empty bed where she'd spent weeks recovering. Nurse Dianna stood behind her, patted her on the shoulder, then wheeled her out through the doorway and down the hall.

"Don't worry, love. You'll do so much better in rehab. It's far nicer than this old place."

Milly looked up at her from the wheelchair, and the nurse winked.

Milly laughed. "You're just trying to make me feel better."

"Not at all. The food will be divine compared to what you've been eating here." The nurse pushed her into a lift and hit the button for the ground floor.

"It can't be worse," Milly quipped.

Despite her reluctance to work with Callum on that first

day, in the weeks since, she'd done what he asked without arguing too much. And she had to admit that it felt good to move, even though she wasn't doing much. Lying in bed all day had gotten old, and she was ready to transition to the rehab facility, although she was still terrified of not having the nursing staff and doctors on call to take care of her.

"Will the staff at rehab check on me regularly?" she asked, her voice shaking a little even though she was doing her best to seem nonchalant about the whole thing.

Nurse Dianna stopped the wheelchair before the wide sliding doors and stood in front of her. She took Milly's hands into her own and looked into her eyes. "They'll take very good care of you. You're going to be fine. No, not just fine. You'll be great. I can't wait to hear about how well you're doing."

Once Milly was in the van, she waved goodbye to Nurse Dianna. Her throat tightened, and she stared down at the mobile phone clenched tightly in one hand. She hadn't heard from Hannah in days, and Callum wasn't scheduled to work with her again until she was settled in her new accommodations. She felt very alone.

With a sigh, she dialled Hannah's number and drummed her fingers on the van window while she waited. It took a while, but Hannah finally answered.

"Hello, love. How are you today?"

"It's moving day. I'm headed over to rehab. I thought you might come."

"Huh? Oh, you're moving? Sorry, love. I forgot all about that. When did you tell me?"

Milly's eyes narrowed. "I mentioned it a few days ago. I've been trying to call, but you weren't answering. Is everything okay, Hannah?"

Hannah coughed, a loud hacking sound that almost deafened Milly. She held the phone away from her ear in alarm. "Are you sick?"

"Oh, I'm fine. Don't worry yourself about me, honey. I don't always hear the phone. Darned thing is so quiet, and then even when I do hear it, sometimes I can't find it. You know how it is."

It worried Milly to hear Hannah talk this way. She shouldn't have neglected her in recent years. Why hadn't she stayed in touch? Hannah had needed her — something she'd never thought about. It'd always been Hannah who'd been there for Milly. Hannah who helped Milly when she needed it. Hannah who had the comforting words and the warm meal, who made Milly feel better when things in her life were hard. But what had Hannah needed from Milly?

It was true that the young were selfish, and Milly was only just beginning to realise how selfish she'd been.

"I'm sorry I wasn't there for you," she whispered.

"What's that, love? I can't hear you over the blasted TV. I'm looking for the remote to turn it down, but it's vanished into thin air."

"Have you been struggling with your memory lately?" she asked as the van pulled away from the curb and turned out of the hospital driveway onto the main road.

Hannah coughed again. "I guess you could say that. The doctor says I have dementia, but I don't think there's anything they can do about it. It's not too bad yet, but I do forget things. And I find that utterly annoying. I always had a good memory. But now, things don't stay in my head for long, I'm afraid. And it drives me batty. Now, why were you calling, love? Did you need something?"

After Milly had reassured Hannah that she didn't need anything and she'd call again later, she hung up the phone and leaned back against the seat. She stared out the window, still holding tight to the phone in her hand.

Hannah had dementia. It hit her hard. What would that mean? Would she forget who Milly was soon? Or did it take longer than that? Was anyone caring for Hannah? She tried to recall if Hannah had any family, or if the foster kids she'd raised were all she had. There was a brother somewhere nearby, but they didn't seem to be very close. If he was still alive, he'd be as elderly as Hannah. She should investigate, find out who was looking after her foster mother. It was the least she could do.

Then it struck her with a pang of shame—it was the *only* thing she could do. Even if Hannah needed care and had no one else to do it, Milly wasn't capable. She needed someone to look after her—she couldn't care for another person. She squeezed her eyes shut tight and pressed a hand to her mouth to stifle a groan. Why rebuild her life? The one person she cared about needed her, and she couldn't do anything to help.

———

"Dinner is at five thirty. I'll show you the dining room later, if you want to try to make it there. Otherwise, you can opt to eat in your room, although I encourage you to join the group and make friends. You'll be here a while, and it's important to connect with the other residents."

The nurse who wheeled her around the facility, pointing out the games room, the TV room, and the residents' bedrooms, had a large gap between her front teeth. When she smiled, it lit up her whole face, and her dark eyes were warm and friendly as she studied Milly for a few moments. She turned to pull open the blue curtains that hung at the single window on the opposite wall.

Milly's room was small, but at least it was private, something she hadn't had at the hospital. It looked cozy enough, with a blue quilt on the bed and a framed picture of a blue flower on the wall beside it. The nurse helped her out of the wheelchair and into the bed. She showed her the call button and the TV remote. All Milly could think about was how alone she felt.

"Would you like me to get anything for you?" the nurse asked.

"I'm tired. I think I'll take a nap."

With a nod, the nurse left the room, and Milly lay back on the soft pillows with a sigh. How long would she be here? Would her life ever be her own again? If she did leave, what would she do and where would she go?

If she let herself think too long, it sent her into a spiral. She had so many questions, and yet there were no answers. She knew the danger of letting herself fall into a pit of despair, but she couldn't seem to keep it from happening because she had nothing to hold on to any longer.

CHAPTER
Eight

I'm on the road. The tarmac is hot against the soles of my feet. Burning hot. And the smoke is thicker this time. I know it's a dream because I've been here before. But I can't seem to get myself to wake up. I'm hungry, I'm afraid, but I know it's not real. So instead of walking, this time, I look around.

Where am I?

There's nothing to give me a hint of my whereabouts other than the fact that the bush is dry, but not outback dry. There are trees, lots of them. Mostly gum. And they're tall and straight. So, I'm not near the beach, and I'm not in the outback. I'm somewhere in between, although that doesn't narrow it down much given the size of Australia.

It's hot where I am. I can tell because there are streaks of dirty sweat on my pudgy little arms. I cough, and it feels like my lungs are being squeezed tight by some unseen hand. The smoke is too thick. I'm going to suffocate if I don't get out of here. Panic rushes over me in a wave. Then it's gone again, and I strain my neck looking for the car. It has to be coming soon. Surely?

I glance back over my shoulder, and there's something in the distance. A dark figure. A person. My heart leaps at the sight. Is it my mother or my father? I don't know, but it feels like they're there.

I turn and start toddling in that direction. I move off the tarmac to keep my soles from blistering, and now the sharpness of the gravel tears into my flesh with each step.

I whimper but keep going. I have to reach them.

But the figure moves away. They haven't seen me. They don't know I'm there. I try to call out, but my voice won't cooperate. There's no sound but for the crack of burning timber.

Embers float through the air and land on the road around me. Smouldering orange and red, they turn black as soon as they land. One lights on the tip of my nose, and I dash it away with one hand. I have to keep moving. I've got to catch up to them.

They're gone. I don't know where they went, but there's no figure ahead of me now. Only thick smoke, getting blacker by the moment.

Then the car is there. I don't remember hearing it pull up nearby, but when I turn away from the smoke, it's there. And the woman is already standing beside it. She hurries towards me. I know the questions she's going to ask. I look up at her, searching for answers. Who is she? Where did she come from? What happens after I get into her car?

I don't have the answers to any of these questions, and I can't ask. My voice seems stuck in my chest.

She reaches down and scoops me up. Holds me against her shoulder and carries me towards the car. I look back and see the figure in the smoke.

"Mum!" I cry out, the sound sending a jolt of surprise through me. "Mum!"

———

WHEN MILLY WOKE, it was to the sound of someone knocking gently on her door. Her entire body was bathed in sweat. The heaviness of the dream still hung in the air around her. She rubbed the sleep from her eyes. What time was it?

The clock on the bedside table said it was nine am. She

hadn't slept that late since the accident. She was hungry, which was a good sign. Her appetite had been progressively improving. What she desperately wanted was some chocolate but her doctor had expressly forbidden it — it wouldn't help with her recovery, he'd said. She had to focus on eating nutritious food and forget about junk for a while. *It's not forever,* he'd stated. But it certainly felt that way to her. It seemed like she'd lived in the hospital her entire life, some days. And her sleep patterns were all over the place.

The hospital had been full of noises — the lift dinging, people talking, nurses scurrying here and there, babies crying. It never ended. But the only thing she heard as she pushed herself into a seated position was birdsong outside her window and another gentle tap on the door.

"Who is it?" she asked.

Callum poked his head through the doorway. "I'm here for our training session. Are you ready?"

She shook her head and yawned. "I'm not quite awake."

He smiled. "I'll get the nurse and meet you in the gym. Okay?"

The nurse who came to help her to the bathroom was a younger woman than the one the previous afternoon. She had ginger hair and a rosebud mouth.

"My name's Mary. I'll be around all day, so you can call if you need anything."

"Thanks," Milly replied. She already felt better than she had the night before. She'd slept so deeply, she didn't recall waking at all. In the hospital, she'd woken at least once per hour. She was refreshed, and her head wasn't so clouded.

"You let me sleep late," she said.

The nurse laughed. "It's your first day. Besides, I came in at seven to wake you and you wouldn't budge. I think you needed it."

"I didn't realise how tired I was."

"It's hard to sleep in a hospital. You'll get more rest now

that you're in rehab. We'll have you feeling like yourself again in no time."

"Apart from this," Milly said, tapping her legs with her fingertips.

"You'll find a new normal," Mary replied gently. "It's a process. But we're here to help you find your way."

Milly bit back a retort. She didn't want false hope, but she also didn't feel like starting a fight. Besides, she had to ready herself for the training session with Callum. Even thinking about it made her heart race. She wasn't ready to train the way he expected her to, and it frustrated her to no end that he wouldn't back down. He wanted to push her and seemed to have no concept of just how injured she was, that she couldn't do it. Why wouldn't he listen?

Mary helped her get ready and then wheeled her down to the gym. Milly had tried to talk her out of it. She mentioned she had a tickle in her throat, and it probably wasn't a good idea to train when she was most likely under the weather. But Mary had laughed at that and replied she wasn't training for a marathon. Likely Callum just wanted to do some simple exercises with her.

"Humph," Milly replied. "You don't know Callum." There was no chance he'd let her get away with a light workout. He was a taskmaster, and she had no power over him. She was accustomed to being able to get people around to her way of thinking, to elicit some kind of sympathy or compassion from them so she could get her own way. But not with Callum. He seemed completely oblivious to how she might be feeling or what she might need. He was selfish, she decided. Selfish and stubborn.

Down a long hallway with rooms on either side, the gym was a large space with double doors that opened automatically to allow wheelchair access. Inside, she saw Callum stacking weights in the corner. He wore a grey T-shirt with a

V-neck and a pair of soft black shorts. His hair was damp, and his skin was tanned.

Milly thanked the nurse, who left her inside the door. She felt awkward. There was only one other person in the gym. An older man on a treadmill, headphones over his ears as his eyes focused on a television screen that hung from the ceiling in front of him.

Callum walked over to her, a smile on his face. "You ready to go?"

She sighed. "I guess. Do I have a choice?"

"You always have a choice. But if you want to heal, you've got to put in the work." He frowned. "Let's start with something simple."

They spent the next half hour with Callum helping her lift small hand weights, followed by abdominal work on the floor mat. He picked her up as though she was as light as a feather and set her down gently on the floor. Then he massaged her feet and calves while explaining the exercises to her. She found it difficult to balance herself, having spent weeks lying on her back and with no strength from her legs to keep her upright, although she had experienced some sensation in both legs in recent days, a fact she'd kept to herself. It'd started with her left toe itching, and she'd twitched it involuntarily. The movement had seemed so natural that at first she hadn't really noticed. And when she tried to repeat the twitch, she couldn't.

"You seem to be sitting up okay. How are your legs? Any movement?"

She shook her head. She wasn't ready to tell Callum about the sensation she'd felt. It had only been in her toes, and it wasn't much. Certainly nothing to get excited about. What would be the purpose in raising her own hopes, as well as his, for something so trivial?

When she could do no more and was gasping for breath, Callum helped her back into her chair and settled onto a weights bench in front of her. He studied her for a moment. "Everything okay with you?"

She laughed bitterly. "Apart from this?" She gestured towards her useless legs and the wheelchair beneath her.

She tucked a strand of hair behind her ear. The way he watched her was unnerving. He looked at her as though he cared, but he didn't know her. Why would he care about her? She was just another one of his clients. He probably complained about her to his girlfriend.

Callum spoke softly. "Yes, apart from that. Or if you want to, we can talk about the challenges you're facing. Whatever's on your mind."

"What's on my mind?" She shook her head. Where to begin? There were so many things trawling through her thoughts at any given moment, she was exhausted by it all. "Let's see… What's on my mind? I don't know. How about the fact that I'm twenty-six years old and I may never walk again? Or the fact that my boyfriend of five years broke up with me as soon as the doctor shared the news with us?"

"It's hard, I know." Callum's brown eyes were soft with compassion.

She shrugged. "It's…whatever. I'm used to people leaving. What really bothers me is how I'm going to live. My job is physical. I can't go back to it. I don't have enough money to support myself for long without work. So, what do I do?"

"I'm sure the government will help…"

"I don't want to live that way," she snapped, her jaw clenching to fight against the emotion welling up from deep within. "I don't need them. I don't need anyone."

He sighed. "You're angry. I get it."

"You have no idea," she whispered.

"I may not know what it's like to experience your life and struggles, but I've had a few of my own. I understand how difficult it is. But it sounds to me like you're giving up, and you can't do that."

"Why not?" she muttered, all the fight draining from her body. "What difference does it make?"

"Because you've got a chance to build a life for yourself. It might look different to how you thought it should, but that boyfriend of yours was a waste of your time and energy, and now he's gone. Good riddance. You don't need people like that in your life."

He had a point. She might've kept dating Kevin for several more years before she gave up on him. She wasn't good at intimacy, but she was great at staying connected to people long after she should've walked away. Anything to stave off the loneliness.

"You'll need a new career, but that's not the end of the world. Most people change careers a few times throughout their life. You're just doing it a little earlier, that's all. There are plenty of things you can do. I'm sure you're talented in ways you haven't even discovered yet. Give yourself a chance."

He helped her back to her room in silence. Neither one of them spoke other than to say goodbye. As he walked away, Milly sat in her chair waiting for the nurse to come, her throat tight. If she listened to Callum and let hope creep back into her heart, it would hurt even more than it already did. She'd managed to get as far as she had by keeping her emotions in check, by not expecting anything more than she had. It was all she could do to get through each day. But maybe he was right. She simply didn't know how to open her heart.

CHAPTER
Nine

CALLUM CLICKED the button on the television remote, and the screen sprang to life. A TV show he had no interest in whatsoever played across the screen, and he stared at it without seeing it. His flat was too quiet. He'd already taken a run this morning. He'd spent all day working in Brisbane with his various clients. He was tired and needed to relax. He'd had a roommate for most of his life—his parents, his brother, military buddies, police colleagues. He still hadn't gotten used to living on his own. He didn't much like it.

There were some advantages, of course. He never had to put the toilet seat down, unless guests came over, which was rare. And he could keep whatever food he wanted in the fridge — even smelly curries or the fish he'd caught that morning and filleted by the waterside. There was no one to tell him what to do or to complain over the mess. But the truth was, he wasn't messy, and he missed having someone around to talk to. If he was back in Rockhampton, he would've called Brad to hang out. But here in Palm Beach, he was completely alone.

He picked up the phone and dialled. Brad answered after three rings.

"Mate! How are you?"

He smiled at the sound of his friend's voice. "I'm good. You?"

"Great. Just about to start a shift."

"I won't keep you. I thought I'd catch up. It's been a minute."

"How are the golden beaches? No, don't tell me. I'll only be jealous."

"It's pretty idyllic, I have to admit." Callum laughed. "But I miss you. All of you. The whole crew."

"We miss you too, mate. But you're doing bigger and better things. You'll figure it out. It takes time to adjust to something new, but give yourself a chance."

Callum considered the irony of his friend's words. He'd given this same speech to Milly earlier that day. Of course, he hadn't considered applying his pep talk to his own life. But Brad was right.

"How's the work going?" Brad asked, as though reading his mind.

"It's pretty interesting. I feel like I'm in over my head most of the time, though. There's this one client — a young woman. She's had a horseback-riding accident and can't use her legs."

"That's hard," Brad replied.

"Yeah, it is. And she's really struggling. I can't stop thinking about her, actually. She hasn't told me much about her life, but her boyfriend left her when the doctor spoke to them about her prognosis. And she hasn't mentioned any family. I think she's all alone."

"Wow. I'm glad you're there to help."

"I am too," Callum replied. And for the first time in months, he felt a sense of purpose. He wasn't lost or floating adrift. His life had meaning. He could help people who had no one else on their side. Milly might be alone in the world, but he would do whatever he could to help her find a way forward.

After he hung up the phone with Brad, he changed into running clothes and headed out. But this time, he turned away from the beach and towards the centre of town. Palm Beach was a busy suburb of the wider Gold Coast city. The traffic flowed steadily in both directions on the main road outside his flat. The scent of salt hung in the hot air. Seagulls fought over a fallen packet of chips beside an overflowing rubbish bin.

Callum broke into a jog. He'd need to find himself a social life or he'd end up a marathon runner. The thought made him laugh to himself as he crossed the road at the lights. On the other side, he stopped to wait for the lights to allow him to cross a busy side street. There was a petrol station opposite, and he had an urge to buy a large iced coffee. He didn't treat himself often, but when he did, an iced coffee with a meat pie was his go-to indulgence.

Beside him, a woman jogged in place, earbuds dangling slightly from her ears. She tipped her head to one side, then the other, stretching out her neck. Dark glasses obscured her eyes. Just then, she stepped out over the curb. A truck turned the corner. Callum reached out and grabbed her by the arm, tugging her back onto the pavement just as the truck roared past.

The woman gasped and stumbled. Callum helped steady her. She lifted her sunglasses and perched them on top of her head. "I thought the light had changed."

"Not yet," he replied.

She pressed a hand to her chest. "Thank you so much."

"No worries."

The light changed then, and they both jogged across and headed in different directions. He walked into the petrol station, his spirits lifted. There wasn't much he liked more than knowing he'd helped someone. It gave him a sense of satisfaction. It was probably why he'd gone into the military and then the police force. But over the years, he'd lost sight of why. There was so much chaos in policing. So many hurt and broken people. It had become impossible for him to see a way forward, like nothing he did really mattered. But now he had an opportunity to really make a difference in the lives of his clients.

He purchased the iced coffee, and then a meat pie from the small oven on the counter. It was crispy and hot when he took it from the paper wrapping. He stood outside and took a bite, then quickly gulped down a mouthful of iced coffee when it burned his tongue.

"Callum?"

He spun around to find his boss, Ted, striding across the pavement towards him. "Hi, Ted."

"Just getting some petrol and I saw you standing here." Ted pressed his hands to his hips and grinned at Callum.

"I was hungry."

"That smells great. Now I'll have to get one too. I'm starving."

"I'll wait if you like."

"Okay. Just be a minute."

Ted disappeared into the shop, then returned a few minutes later with a pie and drink of his own. The two of them wandered to a nearby picnic bench and sat on opposite sides.

"I've been meaning to have a chat with you about work," Ted began as he peeled the paper away from his pie. "I like to catch up with people every week or so, see how things are going."

"I think it's going well so far," Callum replied before taking another bite of pie. The pastry was flaky and melted in his mouth. The meat was soft and covered in a thick gravy.

"How are the clients?"

"Most of them are pretty straightforward, I think. But Amelia Wilson is proving to be a bit challenging."

"It's a difficult case, for sure. I know you're new to using physical training as therapy, but since you majored in it, I thought this might be a good one to try out your skills."

"I'm grateful you gave the case to me," Callum replied. "I would love to run a few things by you and get your take."

"Okay, shoot." Ted swallowed a mouthful of cola.

"She's angry, which I suppose is to be expected. I don't know if she's receiving any therapy—I should probably ask about that. But she seems to need it. She doesn't want to do the workouts. She's reluctant to have any hope at all about regaining function in her legs."

"Is it possible? What do her doctors say?"

"From what I understand, there's a good chance. But she won't work with me to see if we can make progress there."

Ted thought for a moment, his brow furrowed. "It's normal for her to go through the stages of grief. Rage is one of those stages. And maybe she's stuck there. But it's your job to get her to step out of that and to give herself the best possible chance she can."

"And how do I do that?" Callum asked.

"You'll have to judge that for yourself. Depending on her personality, it might involve tough love or a gentle approach. No one can tell you exactly what you should do. You'll have to get to know her and find out what makes her tick. Every-one's motivated by something — whether love, fear, competi-tion or money. We all have a trigger. You simply have to find hers."

Callum grunted. "Simple, huh?"

"It's not easy, but I know you can do it. You've got great instincts."

"Do I? I'm not so sure sometimes."

"I haven't known you long, but already I can see you're the kind of man who cares. And you spent enough time on the force to understand people and how they operate. Rely on your instinct. It'll tell you how to get on her good side. If you still don't make any progress, we'll come up with a different plan at our next catch-up. Does that sound okay?"

"Yeah, thanks. I think I just needed to know that I'm on the right path. It's so ambiguous."

"Unfortunately, there's no one to tell us exactly how to get through to people. It's something we have to figure out on the journey."

"Thanks, Ted. It helps more than you realise."

"You'll be fine. Keep doing what you're doing. I know you'll find a way."

CHAPTER
Ten

"I THOUGHT we'd do something different today."

Milly rolled her eyes. Callum was particularly perky, and she was resisting the urge to laugh along with him. His smile was contagious, although she'd never admit that to him.

She huffed. "Like what?"

"Let's take a walk."

"Are you serious? Hello?" She shook her head. "I think you've forgotten a fairly essential part of my situation."

He sighed. "I mean, I'll walk and push you. Or you can practice controlling the wheelchair yourself. Either way, I thought it might be nice for you to get out and about and see something outside of this rehab facility. I've already gotten approval from your medical team and signed you out. And we can take my car."

It would be nice to go outside. She hadn't done anything remotely interesting in months. She'd even gotten sick of watching television, something she'd previously believed impossible.

"Let's go, then," she said with a shy smile.

He grinned and reached for the handles on her chair. "I'll drive."

"You're hilarious. Did anyone ever tell you that you're too young for dad jokes?"

He grunted. "I'm thirty-two. That's old enough for dad jokes in my book."

She'd secretly wondered how old he was but hadn't wanted to ask. Sometimes he acted like he was eighteen and other times he seemed like an eighty-year-old, so it was hard for her to guess.

"Why aren't you married?" she asked.

He pushed her through the automatic doors and into the sunshine. "That's a random and very personal question. I was engaged last year, but it didn't work out."

"I'm sorry."

"It's no big deal. Turned out for the best. Wait a moment and I'll open the door, then slide you into the front seat. Okay?"

"I can't tell you how much I love relying on someone else for every single move I make," she said with a sniff.

"Sarcasm again?"

"How'd you guess?"

He shook his head as he opened the passenger door. "You don't have to be like that with me. Just relax. We're gonna have some fun."

Be like what? She didn't bother to ask. She'd used sarcasm her entire life. It was part of who she was. Did he expect her to change everything about herself? Become a whole different person? Just when she'd begun thinking he wasn't so bad, he went and irritated her all over again.

He bent low and scooped her up sideways. She slipped one arm around his neck. He smelled like salt and cologne.

"So, where are we going?"

"It's a surprise," he said as he shut the door.

He put her wheelchair in the back of his truck and tied it down. Then he climbed into the driver's seat.

"Hold on to your hat."

She laughed as he accelerated away from the curb.

————

Callum drove south for about an hour and a half. They listened to music and talked about their favourite bands. They discussed books and what she was reading. He asked if he could borrow the thriller she'd just finished, and she offered to give it to him when they got back to the rehab centre. They didn't talk about anything serious, and it was the first time in months she had been able to forget for a moment that her life was in ruins. For the length of the drive, she was just a woman, driving with a man, talking about nothing in particular and enjoying the fresh air blowing on her face through an open car window.

Callum pulled over to the side of the road.

"Where are we?" she asked.

"Cabarita," he said. "I'll be back in a few minutes."

He climbed out of the car in front of a small restaurant with a sign that read *The Stunned Mullet*. He soon returned with a package wrapped in paper. The divine scent of hot chips and freshly fried fish fillets filled the car as he set the package on her lap.

"That smells amazing," she said, inhaling deeply. "Oh, wow. I've missed that so much."

"You from the beach originally?"

"I spent some of my childhood in Palm Beach."

"That's where I live," he replied, surprise in his voice. "What are the chances?"

"Well, I wasn't there long. Only a few years. The rest of my childhood, I was in Brisbane, various suburbs."

"Did you enjoy it?"

She huffed. "Enjoy foster homes? No, not really. I survived it, which is something, I guess."

He sat in silence for a few minutes as they drove along a

winding road beside the ocean. She glanced back over her shoulder and caught a brief glimpse of a sweeping beach beside a jagged cliff. The view was breathtaking.

"Wow," she whispered.

"Pretty nice, huh? Let's stop here. There's a lovely coastal walk with a footpath." He pulled into a parking space and helped her into her chair.

She held the package of fish and chips while he pushed her along the footpath. Before long, they were in front of the view she'd seen while they were driving. It was just as spectacular as she'd thought the first time she saw it. They settled around a picnic table, her in her chair, him on a bench seat beside her. They were on top of a tall cliff face, with only a narrow fence between them and the fall. Below the cliffs, the azure waters pounded white and frothy against a shimmering beach that stretched to the horizon.

"It's so beautiful here," she murmured, forgetting about her growling stomach for a few moments.

"I love it. I sometimes come here to think." Callum tore open the paper and displayed two long golden fish fillets on a stack of hot, salty chips. "Let's eat."

The first bite was heavenly. The soft, flaky fish was perfectly warm and lightly fried. She crunched on the breading and reached for a thick chip. "I don't know how long it's been since I've had fish and chips. I forgot how much I love it."

"You've got to eat it every now and then so you can remember how great life is."

She laughed. "I didn't realise you were such a poet."

"I've got all kinds of hidden talents," he replied, his eyes twinkling.

She liked this side of him. "That sounds like a challenge."

"If you like."

She laughed. "Tell me something about yourself."

"Okay." He paused to take a bite. "I was in the military."

"I already knew that." She shook her head.

"Yes, but let me finish. I specialised in defusing bombs. So, I spent a lot of my time in Afghanistan hoping I wouldn't be blown to pieces."

"Wow. That's kind of morbid."

"Yep." He reached for a chip and popped it into his mouth. "After a while, you get pretty cavalier about the whole thing. Not that I wanted to die or anything, but you can't keep living in that kind of stress without learning to adapt to it."

"Did it ever go wrong?"

"Yes, once." His face darkened.

"You don't have to talk about it," she said quickly. "How about the police force? Did you keep working on bombs?"

"They wanted me to, but I had no desire to continue that line of work. Besides, I wanted to live near my parents in Rockhampton, and there's no bomb squad there. So, I became a detective."

"Robbery? Murder? That kind of thing?" she asked, reaching for another chip.

"That's right. It was a lot less stressful than bombs, but still not exactly a day at the beach."

She hadn't taken the time to think about what he might've been through. She'd been so caught up in her own self-pity, she hadn't stopped to consider who he was and what his life had been like. "And your parents? Are they still up there?"

"No," he replied. "They moved down here, but now they're traveling around Australia in their caravan, so I don't see much of them. But I'm hoping we'll see more of them when they come home. Maybe they'll travel forever. They've definitely got the travel bug."

"So, you're on your own then?" She wanted to take the words back as soon as they came from her mouth. It wasn't her business, and she hated to get too personal with anyone. Loneliness was something she was intimately acquainted with, and it wasn't the kind of lighthearted conversation to have with someone she barely knew. Someone who was her personal trainer and who drove her crazy more often than not.

"I'm on my own," he admitted without any hesitation. "My friends are still in Rocky. But I've got some nice colleagues I'm working with, and I'll find my community eventually. It just takes time." He sounded as though he was trying to convince himself as he spoke.

"I'm sure you will," she encouraged him.

They finished eating, and Callum pulled a small package out of his pocket. "Now, don't tell the nursing staff, but I got you some chocolate." He winked.

She took the small bar of chocolate and gazed at it. "This is the best day ever."

He laughed, his lips pulled wide. "I thought chocolate might be just what you needed today. Now, let's take that walk."

She couldn't wipe the smile from her face as he pushed her along the footpath. A light breeze brushed her skin, and the sun was warm on her face. Some seagulls glided in the sky overhead and others fought for the scraps of chips they'd left behind on the table with loud squawks and violent flapping of wings. A hawk circled high above, almost like a speck in the blue expanse.

He pushed her chair up a slight hill to a half-circle lookout on the top of the cliff. Then he stopped and put the brakes on her chair, and moved the footrests aside.

"Will you trust me?" he asked, reaching for her.

She didn't say a word, but looped her arms around his neck. His hands slid around behind her and lifted her from the chair until she was standing in front of him, pressed up against his body.

"Callum…"

"It's okay. I've got you," he said as he scooped her up and

carried her to the edge of the lookout. He set her down so she was facing out, with her hands resting on the top rail. Then he held her from behind so she could feel as though she was standing on her own.

Tears pricked the corners of her eyes. It was more than she could've imagined. Life coursed through her veins. She closed her eyes, raised her face, and took in a deep breath. Her lungs filled with sweet salty air. She blinked her eyes open again, then let her gaze wander over the ocean, the cliffs, the black rocks at their base and the dots of people swimming and surfing below.

There was a twitch in one of her feet. She felt the pebbles beneath them through the soles of her sandals. There was a slight pain in her right calf.

"I feel it," she cried.

"Feel what?" Callum asked. "Are you okay?"

"My feet. I feel the sandals, and there's some pain in my calf. I can feel my feet and my lower legs."

He carried her back to the chair and lifted her into it, then knelt to remove her sandals. He massaged her feet gently with his hands, moving up to her calves and then back again. "How does that feel?"

She laughed. "It feels good."

"You have sensation?"

She nodded. "I do."

He grinned. "That's fantastic."

She leaned forward and wrapped her arms around his neck, pressing her cheek to his. "Thank you. I don't know what else to say, but thank you."

"This is all on you," he said. "I didn't do anything. Your body is healing on its own."

"But bringing me here… I feel so much better."

"I'm glad. I hoped some fresh air and sunshine might help."

They stayed for a while until she thought she might be

sunburned. Then Callum wheeled her back part of the way and she managed it herself for the rest of the way. She tired quickly whenever she faced a hill in her wheelchair. Her arms had gotten stronger over the weeks, but there were still times she needed help. Inside the truck, she sat in silence, smiling over what had happened. As Callum climbed into the driver's seat and started the engine, her phone rang. She pulled it out of her pocket and answered.

"Hello. This is Milly."

"Amelia Wilson?" A strange voice asked the question.

She glanced at the screen. The name read *Mama*, but the voice wasn't her foster mother's.

"Yes, that's me."

"Hi, I'm Will Templeton. I'm a solicitor out of Palm Beach. I'm afraid I have some bad news. Hannah Bigsby passed away two days ago. I'm going through her phone to contact everyone on her list and let them know. I'm so sorry for your loss."

Milly gasped. "What? How? What happened?"

"Heart attack, I'm afraid. It happened fast. She didn't suffer. There'll be a funeral next week. I'll text you the details, if you'd like."

"Thank you. That would be good." She hung up the phone and stared unseeing at the dashboard in front of her.

"What's happened?" Callum asked quietly.

"It's my foster mother. She had a heart attack and died two days ago."

"I'm so sorry, Milly." Callum rested a warm hand on her shoulder.

She inhaled a slow breath. "I can't believe it. I saw her only last week. She didn't look good, but she assured me everything was okay. And I was so caught up in my own problems, I didn't push. I tried calling her yesterday, but she didn't answer. I can't… I don't know what to…" She pressed both hands to her face. This couldn't be happening.

"The funeral is next week," she said. "In Palm Beach. But I have no way of getting there."

"I can take you," Callum replied.

"You don't have to do that," she said with a shake of her head. "That's not part of your job."

"I don't mind. It's fine. I'm happy to do it."

CHAPTER
Eleven

"I THOUGHT you might like to know. That's all." Milly held the phone to her ear as she gazed out across the gardens surrounding the rehab facility from the comfort of her chair.

"Thanks. I'm sorry. I don't really know what else to say."

She'd called Kevin to tell him about Hannah's death days ago but hadn't been able to reach him. He'd finally answered, but now that she was speaking to him, she wondered why she'd felt the urgency. She hadn't expected him to pick up, since he'd cut ties so completely. There was nothing between them any longer. Any remaining spark of affection she'd had for him had gone, and he seemed to feel much the same way. She suddenly felt very tired.

"That's okay. I'd hoped you might come to the funeral with me, but it's too late now."

"I've got work," he mumbled.

"Right, well… I guess I'll say goodbye, then."

"Bye, Milly. Hope you feel better soon."

She hung up the phone and stared at it a while, then wheeled herself back inside the building. She'd hoped Kevin might come to the funeral with her. She couldn't imagine facing it alone. And yet, now that the phone call was over, she couldn't recall what she'd been hoping for. Of course there was no way he would come. He'd moved on. It'd been over two months since she'd last seen him. He hadn't bothered to call and check on her, and he hadn't sent her a note. There'd been no indication he had any remaining feelings of concern for her at all.

She smoothed the front of her black dress down over her legs. It had been hard to find something to wear, but she'd managed to get into the old dress with the help of the nurse. At least Kevin had shipped some of her belongings to her in a few battered boxes, so she had clothes to wear and her laptop as well as some journals to write in. She was grateful to have something to do with the boundless hours she spent in her room or wheeling around the rehab facility. She'd gotten good at manoeuvring her wheelchair on her own.

As she finished applying mascara, Callum arrived and knocked on her door. She shut the room door behind her and looked up at him with a half smile.

"Let's go."

He stepped behind her and pushed her down the long hallway. "How are you feeling?"

"Odd. Kind of lost. I miss her, but I can't process it fully. I was meant to see her this week. I've been having these dreams, and I wanted to talk to her about them."

"What kind of dreams?"

"I think they're memories, but I'm not sure. She probably wouldn't know what to tell me, of course, since she met me when I was fifteen. But I wanted to talk to her about it all the same."

"I can understand that," Callum replied as he opened the door of his truck and helped her inside.

The sun had climbed halfway up the sky and sat like a molten ball of brilliant light above a puffy white cloud. The heat of the day brought a thin layer of sweat to Milly's forehead. So much for doing her makeup.

"Do you know the way?"

"It's at Saint John's Anglican Church, right?"

"That's right," she replied. "In Palm Beach."

"I've seen it. I think I ran past it the other day."

"I'm sorry you had to drive all the way here, then all the way back again." She felt flustered. She wasn't used to spending time with Callum when he wasn't required to be there. Today wasn't work for him, and she wasn't sure how to act.

"I don't mind. It's my day off, and I had nothing else to do."

"You really should get yourself a life," she replied with a laugh.

He grinned as he started the engine. "Right back atcha."

"Hey!" She shook her head, still smiling. "I have an excuse for the pathetic state of my social life."

"So do I."

"Oh, yeah? And what's that?" She quirked an eyebrow.

He steered out of the driveway and onto the road. "I'm new here, and I'm busy taking care of you. I don't have time for a social life."

"So, what do you do when you're not with me?"

He shrugged. "I run a lot."

"I can believe that." He was the fittest man she'd ever known. He didn't seem to have a single gram of fat on his body.

"Will you know anyone at this funeral?" he asked.

She turned to look out the window, her arm resting on the sill. "I'm sure there will be. I have seven foster sisters."

"Seven?"

"Yep. When I lived with Hannah, she had seven other girls come through at one time or another. Some stayed for a few months, others for years." She hadn't seen any of them lately, although she'd stayed in touch with two of the sisters who'd lived with them the longest.

Emily was a singer who worked retail during the day and did gigs around Brisbane at night. Jonquil was a wedding planner who loved nothing more than helping strangers' romantic dreams of their special day to come true. Milly often wondered how Jonquil had ever become such a romantic given the circumstances of her childhood, but some people stayed pure and hopeful even in the face of hardship and grief. And Jonquil, miraculously, was one of them.

Milly hoped both of the sisters would be there, although she hadn't managed to get either of them on the phone before she left. She wasn't sure she even had the right number for them, given that she hadn't spoken to them in over a year.

"I can't imagine what that must've been like," Callum replied. "I have one older brother, and we're really close."

"Where is he now?"

"He lives in the UK, so we don't see each other often enough, but we talk all the time. He likes telling me what to do and criticising my life choices." He grunted.

"I've never had a big brother, so I have no idea if that's normal."

"It's normal," Callum replied.

"I'll take your word for it."

"So, should I run interference with anyone today? Or will you be okay on your own? I know what these family gatherings can be like. I can guess that the drama only escalates with so many people involved."

"No, it's fine. I don't think there'll be any drama. Everyone loved Hannah. She was a mother to so many of us." Milly swallowed hard. "I just have to get through today."

When they arrived at the church, the parking lot was already jam-packed with vehicles. The church was a single-story brown brick building with a steeple at one end and stained-glass windows on both sides. Callum parked the car and helped Milly into her wheelchair. Then the two of them made their way to the ramp that led to the wide-open double doors on one side of the church.

A deep and heavy sadness settled in Milly's chest when she rolled through the doorway and saw a large photograph of Hannah smiling at the end of the aisle. Usually she chose not to think about her childhood or the years spent shuffling between foster homes. But the sight of Hannah's warm face, several decades younger than she'd been the last time Milly saw her, brought it all rushing back.

"Milly?" A soft voice broke Milly out of her reverie.

Emily stood in one of the pews, wearing a black maxi dress. One arm was looped through the arm of another foster sister, Jonquil. Emily's long chestnut hair hung on either side of her heart-shaped face. Her blue eyes were red-rimmed, and she held a scrunched-up tissue in her free hand.

"Hey, I'm glad you're here," Milly said, wheeling closer.

Jonquil's brown eyes widened. "What…?" She hesitated, confusion lining her pretty face. "Are you okay?"

"I'm fine. I had a horse-riding accident." Milly's cheeks warmed. She'd known it was coming, but the pitying looks were hard to ignore.

"Will you sit with us?" Emily asked, her gaze darting to rest on Callum's face.

"That would be lovely. Thanks." They were seated in the third row from the back of the church. The entire sanctuary was packed, with every seat now taken. "We almost missed out," Milly said, pushing her chair to the end of the pew and out of the way.

Beside her, Jonquil reached for her hand and squeezed it as she sat on the hard timber. "Who's the stud?" she whispered.

Milly laughed. "He's my personal trainer. He's helping me recover from the accident."

"I'll have to find out if he's got any openings," Emily said softly, with a wink. "Although I don't have any money, so that could be an issue."

"I think he only works with rehab clients," Milly replied.

"Shame," Jonquil replied. "Are you okay otherwise?"

The last thing Milly wanted to do was to get into any kind of discussion about her life and prospects. It would depress her even more than she already was, and she couldn't take much more without getting emotional. It was hard enough to face losing Hannah without dwelling on all the other ways her life was spiralling. "I'm fine. Just really sad about Hannah."

"I know. Me too," Emily said, dabbing her nose with the tissue. "I spoke to her last week, and she seemed tired. But I should've said something — told her to go to the doctor. I don't know."

"It's not your fault," Jonquil replied, patting Emily's hand. "You couldn't know. And it was her time. There's nothing you could've done about it."

"I wish I'd done *something* to help," Milly said. "I neglected her."

"We all did," Emily said with a sympathetic look. "I was so caught up in my own life and what's going on with my career. Just paying the bills takes up a lot of my focus. And I tend to get in this tunnel where I can't deal with anything else when I'm anxious or worn out."

"It's been tough lately?" Jonquil asked.

"Making a living writing and singing songs is much harder than you might think." Emily laughed, then wiped her nose again.

"Who could've imagined that?" Milly replied with a smile. "In all seriousness, though, if anyone can make it, you can. You've got so much talent, Emily."

"Thanks, hon. I wish we'd stayed in better contact. With Hannah gone, I'm scared that we'll all lose touch now. And even though we're not officially family, you ladies are all I've got." Emily blew her nose loudly.

Milly's heart ached. She hadn't realised how much she'd missed her sisters until that moment. She looked around the chapel and saw every single one of the girls she'd shared a home with seated in one of the pews, surrounded by others she didn't recognise. She hadn't kept in contact with any of them other than Emily and Jonquil, but she cared about each of them.

"Hey, do you remember that time Hannah caught the three of us eating her Christmas chocolates behind the couch?" Milly asked.

"I felt so bad about that," Emily said with a shake of her head. "She didn't get angry, but said she was disappointed. That was so much worse."

"It was my fault, too," Jonquil added. "I was always hungry. There never seemed to be enough food, and far too many mouths."

"You were growing," Milly replied. "We all were. And Hannah did her best to fill our tummies, but chocolates were definitely our weakness."

"I remember finding the rest of those chocolates in the bottom of our Christmas stockings the next day." Jonquil's eyes glistened with tears. "She didn't eat a single one of them."

"I'd forgotten about that." Images of Hannah's smiling face over a sink full of dirty dishes, or pushing a vacuum cleaner over the carpet with an apron still tied around her ample waist, filled her mind's eye.

"She sang all the time. That's what I remember most," Emily replied, wiping a tear from her eye. "So much music. I'd never known anyone who listened to music all day long like that. I loved it."

The service began then, and Milly focused her attention on

the pastor at the front of the church. He spoke of Hannah's love for her community, the dozens of children she'd helped to raise, the families she'd brought back together. The sanctuary was full of people sniffling and nodding along to the stories he told. Hannah wondered how many of them Hannah had fostered.

After the service was over, they all transferred into a small hall beside the sanctuary where there was finger food and drinks. Callum got Milly a cup of lemonade and a plate of sandwiches. He sat beside her in a folding chair and ate one of the sandwiches from her plate.

"Hannah must've been a wonderful woman," he said.

"She was."

"I'm glad you knew her." He offered her a sympathetic look.

"Have you lost someone you love?"

He swallowed and looked away. "My partner."

"Your…?"

"With the force. We were partners for years. We could almost read each other's thoughts. People assumed we were brothers, and sometimes it felt that way." He smiled. "He died, and I never got to tell him that. I should've done more… said more. I don't know. It's hard to move on when someone's taken unexpectedly like that."

"I'm sorry. That must've been hard."

"Hardest thing I've ever been through. But I made it. My relationship didn't, but that was for the best."

"Your fiancée?"

"Yep. We weren't right for each other. It was time for me to move on. So, here I am. Want another drink?"

"Yes, please."

She watched him walk back to the drinks table. He was a confusing man. Originally she'd thought of him as nothing more than the jock physical trainer who'd been sent to cause her pain. He'd been through a lot and he was far more sensitive than she'd thought. There was a lot more to Callum Montague than her first impression.

Her left toe itched, and she wriggled it. A warm sensation drifted up her leg, and she stared at it in wonder. She'd felt a little more sensation in her legs every day. For the first time in a long time, the anger and bitterness that'd balled inside her shifted, and she felt hopeful.

CHAPTER
Twelve

WHEN THE WAKE WAS OVER, Milly looked for Callum, who'd wandered off. They should leave. He had a life and no doubt things he needed to take care of. She'd already taken up most of his day and he still had to get her back to Brisbane and then drive himself home again.

She wheeled herself out of the hall and down the ramp. An elderly man stood at the bottom of the ramp, shaking hands with people. Jonquil and Emily followed her outside.

"Are you leaving, Milly?" Jonquil asked, shielding her eyes from the glare of the sunshine with one hand.

"As soon as I find Callum." She scanned the group of people who straggled from the church hall to the carpark. She spotted Callum standing in the shade with his phone pressed to his ear. "There he is."

She offered her foster sisters a wan smile.

"I hope we'll see you again soon," Emily said. "I can't believe you didn't call when you hurt yourself. I would've been there to help you."

Milly was surprised. Her sisters had certainly matured in the past few years. She almost didn't recognise them.

"Yeah, me too," Jonquil added. "You've got to stay in touch better. Em and I have dinner once a week. We'd love to include you, if you want to join us."

"That sounds amazing. I'm still in rehab at the moment, but I'm sure they're going to kick me out any day now. I'm able to get around on my own, apart from driving, of course. But I'll stay there as long as they'll let me, since I have nowhere to go."

"Maybe you could room with me, although I'm on the fourth floor, and we don't have an elevator." Jonquil scratched her head.

"That could be an issue. But thanks for the offer. You're the best."

"Stay with me!" Emily declared. "I've got a spare room. My roommate left a few weeks ago, and I was going to live on my own, but I'd love to have you."

"Really? I mean, I wasn't fishing for an offer, so you don't have to…"

"I want you to. I miss having my sisters around." Emily grinned. "Oh, this is going to be great. We'll be roomies again, and we'll have late-night chats and slumber parties every night." She clapped her hands together.

Milly laughed. "I don't know how good I am at slumber parties, but that sounds great."

They meandered down the ramp together to where the grey-haired man was wishing people well on their way out. He wore a blue-and-white checked shirt, buttoned high, and a pair of khaki pants with creases down the front of each leg.

He reached for Milly's hand and shook it with a smile beneath a wide grey moustache. "Thank you so much for coming. I didn't get a chance to introduce myself earlier. I'm Greg, Hannah's brother. And you are?"

"My name's Amelia, but everyone calls me Milly. And this is Jonquil and Emily. We were all foster daughters once upon a time. Hannah took care of us. I'm so sorry for your loss."

His demeanour changed immediately, and he looked thoughtful. "Amelia Wilson?"

"Yes, that's right. Did Hannah mention me?"

He smoothed his moustache with two fingers. "She talked about you a lot. In fact, I was looking for you. There's something I need to speak to you about."

Milly couldn't imagine what Greg might want to say to her. She glanced at Jonquil and Emily. Jonquil shrugged, and Emily gave her an encouraging smile.

"Okay," Milly said.

Greg inhaled a slow breath. "Hannah didn't have much, but she wrote a will and wanted to give the things she had to the people she cared about. She appointed me as executor of her will, and she put everything she owned into a trust so that there'd be no red tape when she died."

"Wow. So, she knew it was coming?"

"She knew," he said with a nod. "She'd been sick for a while. I'm surprised she didn't tell you."

"I asked her a few times if she was feeling okay because she didn't look herself. But she assured me she was fine and it was simply old age." A lump formed in Milly's throat at the memory. Hannah had protected her when she was a teenager and continued doing the same thing until she died.

"That sounds like Hannah," Greg said. "The reason I need to speak to you is that she named you in her will. All three of you, actually. She left Emily her old guitar."

"Oh, I loved that guitar," Emily cried, resting a hand over her heart.

"And she wanted Jonquil to have her coin collection."

Jonquil smiled through a veil of tears. "I used to pore over that collection every day when I was a kid. I thought it would make me rich one day. I made Hannah promise to keep it for me. I can't believe she remembered."

"It won't make you rich, but it's probably worth a little bit," Greg said. "And she left you something more substantial, Milly. She wanted you to have some support in your life, especially since the accident." He looked at the wheelchair, then met Milly's gaze. "She left you her house in Palm Beach."

———

Later that afternoon, Callum dropped Milly back at the rehab centre. She had pondered in silence most of the ride home. He wheeled her to her room and sat in the chair by her bed.

"Want to talk about it?" he asked, steepling his hands together.

"Thanks for driving me."

"You're welcome," he said. "I was glad to be able to be with you. I know it must've been a tough morning. Are you thinking about Hannah?"

The truth was, Hannah was all she could think about. That and the bombshell from Hannah's will. She still couldn't believe it. Why would Hannah leave her a house? A whole house. It was more than Milly could comprehend. She'd never thought she would be able to afford a place of her own even when she was working, but after the accident, she'd been certain that would be an impossibility.

"I spoke to her brother, Greg."

"I saw you talking to someone after the wake. Was that him?"

She nodded. "Hannah left me the Palm Beach house."

"What?" He frowned. "Her house?"

"Remember how I told you I spent some of my childhood living there with her? Now she's given it to me. It's in some kind of trust in my name. Greg says I can move in immediately. He even gave me the keys and said he'd forward the paperwork over as soon as I'm settled."

"That's incredible. Are you excited?"

"I can't take it in. It's too much. Why would she do that? I've hardly seen her in years. It doesn't make sense. She had dozens of foster kids."

"And yet she chose to give her house to you. That says something about how she viewed your relationship, I think." Callum sat on the bed and rested a hand on her shoulder. "You were clearly special to her, and I know you've been beating yourself up about not being there for her, but she clearly wasn't upset about it."

"I hope so." There was nothing she could do to turn back the clock, but the emotions that flooded her, knowing how Hannah, the woman she'd called Mama, had felt such a connection with her, were overwhelming. "She loved me," she whispered, pressing her fingertips to her lips. "If only I could go back and tell her that I love her too."

"She knew," Callum replied, taking her hand and squeezing it with his.

Milly stared at their hands entwined in her lap. His was large enough to envelop hers. It was tanned and strong with thick veins along the back of it, and it felt warm and safe. She was glad he was there with her. But the feelings that rose up from deep within made her uncomfortable. She couldn't let herself need anyone. Not now. Not after being abandoned so many times and by so many people she'd loved.

Everyone but Hannah. Her compassionate act confused Milly. She was too accustomed to being left behind by people like her mother, her father, her other foster parents and even Kevin. She didn't know what to do with a love like the one Hannah had given her — so pure, without expectation. Hannah hadn't wanted anything from Milly, yet had given so much.

"I don't know what to do," she murmured.

Callum released his grip on her hand. She missed the connection, though she'd never admit it to him. "This is great news! You're almost ready to move out. We need to do a bit more PT before I can sign off on the paperwork. I was reluctant to do it when you didn't know where you might go, but now I can process your discharge just as soon as you're ready."

CHAPTER
Thirteen

THE LEVEL of intensity in her workouts increased beyond what Milly had ever thought possible in the weeks that followed. She'd had a moment of affection for Callum, but now he seemed to be doing his best to make her hate him all over again. She couldn't remember ever having endured such pain before in her life as she did during and after one of her training sessions with him. But the silver lining was that she had feeling back in her legs and feet.

When it'd first happened, she'd thought maybe she was imagining things. But the feeling didn't go away. It'd been painful, then aching, and now finally it felt good. Her doctor was hopeful she'd recover full function of her legs, although he wasn't certain how that might look. She could walk, though, he'd assured her. And that had been the best day of her life.

Ever since then, Callum had pushed her to the fringes of her capacity. And when she'd complained, he'd reminded her that they had a goal — to get her out of rehab and moved into Hannah's beach house. It was the image of that house, perched on the edge of Palm Beach, that kept her going even when the pain and effort seemed more than she could bear.

She lifted the weights over her head, her arms shaking with the effort, then set them back in place on the ground beside her. "That's it. I can't keep going. My arms are jelly."

"Now we'll work on your legs. We've got to get you walking soon, so we have to build up the muscle mass that you lost over the past few months."

She wanted to complain, but she didn't have the strength. Instead, she followed his instructions on the leg lifts. It wasn't much, but she managed to get some movement in her legs and feet, and that was better than nothing. She never would've imagined she could draw so much hope from such a little thing as moving her legs, but joy surged up through her chest and made her head light.

"I did it!" she cried, setting her feet back on the ground. "Did you see that? I actually did it."

Callum squatted in front of her, grinning. "Yes, you did. Now, do it again."

"You're a torture merchant." She pouted. "Can't we just celebrate?"

He placed both hands on her knees. "Come on. Let's keep going. You're doing so well. We don't want to lose that momentum."

"But it's good, right?"

"It's great. I'm proud of how far you've come."

"I didn't think I could do it."

"I knew you could."

She smiled at him. "You told me so many times."

"I believe in you."

She'd never had anyone but Hannah believe in her before. It was a strange feeling to know that there was another human in the world who saw potential in her, even more than she did herself. "How did you know?"

"You're a fighter."

Milly laughed. "That much is true. Thank you for believing in me."

"You're welcome."

She was suddenly aware of how close he was. Both hands on her knees, his face hovering only inches from hers. Sweat trickled down her temples and dripped from her chin. She was exhausted down to the very marrow of her bones, yet there was an excitement sending tingles all over her skin. She breathed in the scent of him, cologne and sea salt, her heart racing. His hair was spiked and blond-tipped from swimming in the ocean or running on the beach. He talked often about what he did during his spare time, and she wished for a moment she could do those things with him. It gave her renewed energy, and she pushed her legs up again and again, with him cheering her on.

After their hour together was over, Callum took her back to her room. The doctor was there, studying the chart on her door. He glanced up and gave her a nod.

"There you are. I was about to leave—I'm glad I caught you."

"Hi, Dr Sayed. I've had the most amazing training session. Didn't I, Callum?"

Callum explained to the doctor what she'd achieved in their session, and Dr Sayed seemed suitably impressed. Milly's heart soared.

"That's great to hear, Milly. I think you can expect to be walking in no time. You're improving every day now, and that's what we want to see."

"When will I be able to get back on a horse, Dr Sayed?"

The doctor frowned. "We're not there yet. In fact, at this stage, I would suggest that riding is something you should consider a thing of the past. Walking is the goal. And I'm concerned that if you ride, you might do irreparable damage to your spine. You can't afford another accident. Even the act of riding could be too much."

Milly's face fell. She swallowed hard. Never ride again? She'd thought things would be better now that she had sensation and movement back in her legs. How could he tell her not to ride again? She'd let go of the dream for months, but it'd crept back into her heart in recent days, and she'd been consumed by thoughts of horses and riding in her waking and sleeping hours.

———

When Dr Sayed left the room, Callum watched Milly's reaction go from disbelief to anger and then desperate sadness. Her eyes were large and dark, her hands clenched into fists at her sides. She sat in her chair, slumped over and heaving large breaths of air as though she was in the throes of a panic attack.

"Slow down," he said, helping her onto the bed. She leaned back against the pillows, staring at the ceiling as her eyes filled with big, fat tears. "Take a deep breath."

But she didn't seem to be able to stop the panic from taking over.

"I…can't…breathe…"

He stroked her arm, running his hand slowly down her skin and back up again. "Yes, you can. Breathe, just breathe. Slow it down. Deep breaths. It's okay. Everything's going to be okay."

Her breathing slowed, and she blinked, her cheeks wet. "It's not going to be okay. He said I'll never ride again. Never again! I thought I'd lost that hope months ago, but lately I've been letting it grow again. I can't believe it. After all the work I've done, the pain I've put myself through. Now, I'm back to square one. Alone, with no job, no prospects and hopeless."

He continued stroking her arm, slowly up and down. "That's not true. Don't go there again. You've made so much progress."

"Really? Have I?"

She sat up and swung her legs over the edge of the bed so her knees were pressed up against his stomach. He took a step back. "Yes, you have. Look at you — moving around on your own. Your legs are coming back. Soon you'll be walking again. You have a house of your own now. You didn't know where you'd stay before."

"That's true," she admitted, sniffling. "For a moment, I forgot about the house. I still can't quite believe it's mine. I keep thinking they'll discover the real last will and testament and call me with the bad news."

He shook his head. "You've really got to start thinking more positively."

"You're right. I know you are. I've gotten into this cycle of seeing everything as a potential disaster. I don't know why I do that."

He knew why she did it, and he couldn't blame her. She'd been through so much in her short life. It was hard to understand how she'd come through it as well as she had. She was still so strong, such a fighter. She didn't let things keep her down for long. But she tended to see the glass as half empty, when he could only see possibility and potential.

"You can change your thought patterns. When you find yourself spiralling, exchange those thoughts for positive, affirming ones. Think encouraging thoughts. One of the most important aspects of rehabilitation is for you to have a positive mindset. It impacts the outcome of your recovery more than anything else."

"I want to… I don't know how."

"Give it a try. Let me know how you go."

"Okay, I will," she said. "But I'm sad."

"You can let yourself feel sad. And you should. You've lost something, and it's worth grieving. But only for a few minutes — don't let it spin you into despair."

She stared down at her hands, unclenching her fists and

stretching her fingers. The tears continued falling silently as she sat on the bed, looking so forlorn that it took everything in him to stay at a distance.

She was his client. She was broken, hurting and alone. He couldn't take advantage. It would be wrong. Unprofessional and completely unfeeling. The last thing she needed was for him to bring her more pain, and he'd never had a relationship that didn't end that way. She needed his friendship, nothing more than that. It was all he could give, but it wasn't all he wanted. Not any longer. No matter what happened, whether she walked or never made it out of the chair again, he couldn't help the way he'd begun to feel about her. The attraction grew every time he saw her, but he couldn't tell her that. Couldn't say anything. It wasn't fair to her, and he could deal with the attraction on his own. It was only a crush. He'd had them before and no doubt would again.

She gazed up at him, her eyes glistening with tears. He couldn't take it anymore. He stepped forward and wrapped his arms around her, pulling her close. Her fingers grazed his arms, bringing out the gooseflesh, as she found her place — cheek to chest.

"It'll all be okay. You'll make it through this," he whispered as he raised a hand to stroke her hair gently away from her face.

She sniffled against his shirt. "I know it's silly. If I walk again, that's enough. But I can't help feeling sad over it."

"You hardly ever cry, you should let it out." He'd marvelled over how strong she'd been, the way she used her anger and frustration to express her emotions, but never tears.

"I don't like to cry. But this time…"

He understood. It was the final thing that had pushed her beyond her ability to control herself the way she usually did. "It's good to cry sometimes."

"I don't know about that. I feel horrible." She pulled away and wiped her eyes with the back of one hand.

"You'll feel better soon."

"Promise?" Her gaze found his, and she blinked, her eyelashes wet and black against her pale skin.

"I promise."

THE NEXT DAY, Callum visited the rehab facility. He had three clients there, and it was several hours before he called on Milly. His heart thudded as he stood by her door, waiting for her to answer it. She pulled the door open. He was so eager to see her that he couldn't help grinning. She wore her hair in a long ponytail. Wispy tendrils danced around her face. Big brown eyes looked up at him from where she sat in her chair. Her skin glowed with health and vitality — so different to the woman he'd seen on the first day he'd visited her in hospital.

"Ready to go?" he asked.

She shrugged. "You look extra peppy today."

"I thought we could have an outing again."

"Are we allowed?"

"I asked your doctor, and he's very happy for you to get out and about."

"Where are we going?" She pulled her room door shut behind her.

"We're going to see your new house."

"Really?" A smile drifted across her features. "That's actually a great idea. I've been wanting to go there, see what kind of state it's in. But I didn't think I could. Wait a second. I'll grab the key."

She returned to the room and retrieved her purse. With the purse in her lap, she wheeled herself down the hallway beside Callum. His optimism must've been contagious because he could already tell her mood had risen.

"There's one more thing," he said. "We've been practicing standing, but today you're going to walk."

———

The neighbourhood looked just as she remembered it. Milly leaned against the door of Callum's truck and wound down the window to breathe in the fresh sea air. She let her eyes drift shut and inhaled again, more deeply this time. The air filled her lungs and brought with it a sense of excitement.

Callum laughed.

Her eyes blinked open, and she took in the sights. The long line of beach houses, squatting behind the dunes. The small fish-and-chip shop she couldn't believe was still operating after all these years. The brand-new corner store with its bright red signage beside the old, worn-looking petrol station where she'd escaped many an evening to buy gum or lollies when she'd needed desperately to get away from everyone.

Memories flooded back in. The time Hannah gave her an old second-hand bike with rusty blue paint and she rode it for the first time. She'd wobbled down that side street with feelings of panic and euphoria vying for space in her chest. Or the day she'd first learned how to surf. She'd been trying half-heartedly for months when finally she'd decided she wasn't going inside until she managed to stand up on Hannah's old Malibu board. It'd taken her a dozen tries and more tumbles beneath the waves than she could count before she finally stood. That had been a good day.

Callum pulled the truck into the driveway. He climbed out

and helped her into the chair. It took her a moment to get the key into the lock, but then it turned easily and she was inside. It was a single-story structure, with a large back deck overlooking the dunes and with a view of the beach through the branches of the various trees and bushes that lined the dunes, if she squinted.

She sat in the entryway and inhaled a slow breath. It looked exactly the same. It was as if she'd travelled back in time. The feeling sent goose bumps up and down her arms. There were the same framed photographs of Hannah with her various children on the wall above the hall table. The den was still furnished with the old couches that looked as though they'd been upholstered with some type of velvet carpet. The timber hardwood floors were still scratched and worn in the same places beneath the same Turkish rug she'd purchased on a trip to Istanbul.

"Wow, this is great," Callum said, walking into the kitchen and disappearing from sight. "Have you seen this view?"

She rolled after him. "Of course. I lived here for years."

"That's right—I knew that. What a great place."

"It was the only real home I ever had. At least, that I remember." She rolled gently to the back door. It was a large sliding glass door with floor-to-ceiling windows reaching across the rest of the room where it joined with the deck. "I can't believe she's gone. It feels so strange to be in her house with all her things when she's not here."

Milly glanced around. "I keep expecting her to walk down the hallway and shout that it's been too long and ask why don't I visit more often."

She took Callum on a tour of the house, showed him the bedrooms and bathrooms, the TV room at the other end of the house.

"There's not much to the garden. Hannah loved to grow things, but she wasn't very good at maintenance, so the vegetable garden always looked more like a tiny forest. But I loved gardening, so when I moved in, it was one of the few things I could to do take my mind off things. I'd harvest beans and peas, potatoes and eggplant. She loved that. Always called me her little farmer. And then she'd turn whatever I brought her into some kind of meal that would feed us all. It usually involved pasta or rice to fill it out."

"It sounds like you were happy here."

"I was. I'd been so miserable for so long, I didn't recognise it at first. But by the time I left, I'd had a few good years here and made some lifelong friendships."

Callum reached for one of her hands and stood to his feet. "Okay, enough about memory lane. Later, you can figure out where you're going to put all your things and how your life will look once you're living in this awesome beach house. Right now, it's time to focus. Are you ready to take your first real steps since the accident?"

Her heart fluttered. Was she ready? She'd been waiting for this moment for so long. She'd finally gotten the strength back in her spine. The healing had happened so gradually, she couldn't be sure when she'd realised it was time. But she knew it now with a certainty that pushed a smile across her face.

"I'm ready."

"We really could've done this a few days ago, but I wanted it to be special, and so that's why I hatched a plan to bring you here. This will be your new home, so it's only right that you take your first steps here." He lifted her slowly with both hands beneath her arms. "You can lean on me as much as you like."

At first, all her body weight was in his control. But she gradually shifted until she was standing on her own. Then she lifted one leg. It felt clumsy and heavy, but it moved and she took a step. Callum took a step with her.

"You did it!" he declared, a look of triumph on his handsome face.

She laughed out loud. Then took another step.

"That's amazing. Keep going! You're doing so well." His words of encouragement continued pouring out with every step she took until before she knew it, she'd walked across the whole lounge room and back again.

She fell down onto the couch with a grunt. It'd taken a lot out of her, but she was exhilarated. She puffed from the effort and squeezed her eyes shut for a moment. She had walked. Nothing would be the same again. She could do anything now. The world had slammed shut a few months earlier when she'd fallen, but now it flew open again. She had a future, and it was in large part due to the efforts of the man seated on the couch beside her.

She met his gaze. "Thank you."

He cocked his head to one side, his face awash with compassion and pride. "It wasn't me. You did this. All that work you put into your training sessions has paid off."

"I know I give you a hard time, and I complain a lot about how much pain you put me through. But I couldn't have done it without you."

Reflexively, she covered her abdomen with both hands. Her tummy had grown since she'd been in rehab. The good food plus the mostly inactive lifestyle had caused her previously athletic build to plump up, and she suddenly felt very aware of how close Callum sat to her and just how muscular and slim he was compared with her frumpy, pale and squishy appearance.

"What's wrong?" he asked.

"Nothing." She brushed him off. "Let's try walking again."

"Okay. But first, tell me why the sad look. What just happened?"

Her cheeks pinked. "Can't you let me have some secrets?"

"Of course I can, but it's my job to keep you motivated,

and what I saw for a moment was defeat. I want to know why."

She sighed. "You'll think it's ridiculous. But I'm embarrassed about the weight gain. I've never had a stomach before. I mean, obviously I've had a stomach, but it's always been flat. This…" She prodded at her soft abdomen. "This is different. It's squishy." She screwed up her nose.

He looked down at her hands, then pressed his over the top of them. "You don't have anything to worry about."

"What do you mean? Of course I do. I'm getting fat. All I do is sit around and watch television all day. Well, until you come and put me through the most painful workouts of my life. Other than that, I'm a couch potato. And you look like a Greek god, with your huge muscles and your hard abs. It's embarrassing." Her face was burning with the humiliation of her own words, but it was true. She'd felt ashamed about how her figure was changing for a while but hadn't been able to do anything about it. Truthfully, she hadn't been motivated, either. She'd been down for so long that it was hard to care. But now that things were better, she was walking, she could hope for a full life again, it reminded her that she'd let herself go.

Callum shook his head slowly. "Trust me, you have nothing to worry about."

"But…"

"You'll just have to take my word for it." He cut her off, leaning in close. "I shouldn't say anything more than that because it would be unprofessional."

"Like what? What would be unprofessional?"

He sighed. "You're going to get me into trouble."

"I'd never do that," she quipped, biting down on her lower lip.

He groaned. "Don't bite your lip that way. You're killing me."

"I have no idea what you're talking about, Callum." She tipped her head to one side. "You don't think I'm too fat?"

He huffed. "You know you're hot. You don't need me to tell you that. I'm sure every guy you've ever passed has told you that with the way he looked at you."

"Well… not in a while. And my boyfriend, Kevin, never had many kind things to say about the way I looked. He told me I was too bony and that my cheeks made me look like a squirrel."

"He was clearly a fool." A muscle in his jaw clenched. "I wish I could tell you… But I can't. Because I'm a professional and I'm your trainer. If it got back to my boss that I was flirting with one of my clients…"

"Are you flirting with me?" Milly asked, shocked. She hadn't realised — she'd been so down on herself, she'd become convinced that he must talk to all his clients the way he spoke to her. That she was nothing special to him. That she was fooling herself to think otherwise.

It was his turn for pink cheeks. "Uh… I…" he stammered.

She laughed. This was more fun than she'd had in a long time.

Just then, her phone rang. Annoyed, she pulled it free of her pocket and answered it. "Hello?"

"Can I please speak to Amelia?"

"This is she."

"Oh, hello there, Amelia. It's Greg Bigsby here, Hannah's brother."

"Yes, of course. Hi, Greg. And you can call me Milly."

"Wonderful. I'm glad I caught you, Milly. I understand you have plans to visit the house?"

"Actually, I'm here right now. My trainer brought me over to look around. Is everything okay?" she asked, her heart sinking. It was happening. He'd take it back—she knew the moment was coming.

"Everything's fine. Your trainer called me to let me know.

So, I thought I'd update you — I took a few personal things from the house. Mementoes and so on for the family to keep. Everything else that's still there is yours, if you want it."

"Okay, thanks. I appreciate that."

"If you decide to get rid of anything like photographs or artwork, please let me know so I can decide whether we want to keep it. Otherwise, you're free to do what you like."

"I will definitely keep you in the loop."

"That's great. I know you'll love it there. Hannah would be happy to hear you doing so well."

"Thank you, Greg." Even though she barely knew him, his kindness touched her. There was something familiar about him. He was so much like Hannah.

"And you can call me anytime you need anything at all. Even if it's only to talk. I've got plenty of spare time. You've got my number."

She swallowed around a lump forming in her throat. "That means a lot to me. Thanks. Can I ask, do you know why your sister left this house to me? It's such a big gift. And she had so many people in her life. I'm overwhelmed by it."

He coughed to clear his throat. "Well, she spoke to me about it many times. She talked of you incessantly. Always giving me updates on how you were doing, what was going on in your life, whenever she heard from you. She cared about you a great deal, and she wanted to make sure you were set up."

"It's incredible. I wish I could thank her." Milly shook her head in disbelief. How was this kind of generosity possible? It wasn't something she understood. Although Hannah had always been generous with her and Milly had loved her, she hadn't let anyone else into her heart since.

"The best way to thank her is to thrive. That's what she truly wanted for you."

Milly said her goodbyes and hung up the phone. Callum had moved to the kitchen and was splashing water onto his face when she wheeled herself into the room to see him. He straightened and blinked. "Everything okay?"

"I'm fine. That was Greg."

"I heard."

"He wanted to make sure everything was fine with the house. And he said I could call him anytime." She turned towards the front door. "Let's get out of here. I'm more determined than ever to get ready to move. I can't wait to live here."

CHAPTER
Fifteen

MILLY'S DISCHARGE paperwork was processed. She was leaving rehab that afternoon. Soon she wouldn't need him anymore, and the thought made Callum frown as she pushed the weights up with both hands and then down again. She'd made so much progress, most of it in recent days. Their trip to the new house yesterday had put even more fire in her belly. Their final workout today had been tough, and yet she still wanted more. He'd had to caution her several times not to overdo it.

"What's gotten into you today?" he asked, spotting her as she held the bar over her head and lifted it high again.

Her face was red, and she puffed hard as she set the bar back in place. "I have to get out of here. I'm going mad lying around with nothing to do. I can walk now, so I should be at the house getting my life back on track."

"You're going this afternoon. Isn't that soon enough?"

"Yes, I know." She sat up and swung her legs down on either side of the bench. "I'm nervous, that's all. I haven't been alone in such a long time. I don't know if I can take care of myself."

"Well, you can get groceries delivered, right?"

"Yes, and there's a corner store. I'll be able to walk there before too long, I hope."

"And if you need anything, I'll be close by. We're practically neighbours. I'm only a couple of kilometres away down the beach." He helped her to her feet, and she walked with slow, awkward steps to her chair, then slumped into it with a sigh.

"Walking will never get old," she muttered.

He laughed. "It's pretty incredible. You won't take it for granted again."

As they made their way back to her room for the last time, emotion welled up inside him. Callum wasn't the type of man who generally showed a lot of emotion. He preferred to keep things professional, calm. The approach had always helped him when he was in the military and then later on the police force. But now it was hard to keep his feelings at bay.

He stopped walking when he reached Milly's room. "I'll see you at the house next week."

"You're not coming by sooner?" she asked, looking up at him, eyes wide.

He swallowed. "Our sessions will be weekly now that you're not in the rehab facility. You can continue practicing walking around the house, and I recommend you get an occupational therapist in to look the place over. They might have some recommendations on what you can do to make the house more wheelchair friendly, that kind of thing."

"You sound weird. Why are you talking like that?"

He cleared his throat. "Talking like what?"

"Like you hardly know me."

"Do you need me to help you with anything else?"

She studied him a moment. Then she asked, "Can you help me into the shower?"

His heart skipped a beat. "What?"

She laughed. "Come on, I don't mean it like that. I just need some help. The nurse is nowhere to be seen, and I don't want to stink like this for the rest of the day. I promise not to scandalise you."

"I'm not concerned with being scandalised," he huffed. "Sure, I can help."

He pushed her chair into the room and helped her into the bathroom. Her skin was soft beneath his hands, and he fought against every instinct to pull her close and shut the door behind them. The intensity of his emotions whirled up inside him like a tornado as she brushed up against him, reaching for her towel. She raised her arms over her head and slipped out of her shirt. Now she wore only a pair of bike shorts and an athletic crop top.

He stepped back. "Whoa, wait a minute. I'm leaving."

She faced him, her gaze finding his. "It's okay. I don't mind."

His heart thundered against his ribcage and heat rose through his body at the sight of her. He wanted to grab her, to press his lips to hers. Anything other than this space between them.

She was torturing him. Surely she knew how it would make him feel to be so close to her, yet unable to do anything about the way he felt.

"You really didn't need me for this," he snapped.

"What's wrong? I'm sorry… I didn't think…"

"That's right—you didn't think. You never do. It's all about you, all the time."

She gaped at him, confusion on her face. "That's unfair."

"Look, I'll see you next week. Call me if you need me for anything. Or don't. I don't care."

He slammed the door shut behind him and stormed down the hallway. When he reached the open-air carpark, he leaned against his truck and rubbed his hands over his face. He hadn't meant to lose control that way, but he'd been about to do something that would get him in trouble. He hadn't been in his job long, and if he compromised his relationship with a client, he could get fired. How would he find another job after something like that so early in his career? He wouldn't. That would be the end of everything he'd worked towards for so long. Not to mention the fact that it would break the trust he'd built with Milly over recent months. She'd worked so hard—he couldn't do that to her.

With a sigh, he took one last look at the rehab centre, then climbed into his truck. As he drove away, he pictured the way she'd looked at him, with a mixture of pain, betrayal and innocence on her beautiful face. And his chest ached at the memory.

CHAPTER

Sixteen

FOUR WEEKS LATER, Milly had finally begun to feel at home in her beach house. She couldn't call it a new house, since she guessed it was about thirty years old. It was older than her, in fact. But it was new to her, and she loved it more with each passing day. Every creak it made underfoot, every time the wind whistled through the eaves, every scratch and hole and cobweb was hers. She'd learned to feel a kind of contentment in the past few weeks that was thoroughly new to her. And she wore a half smile whenever she managed to walk between the rooms.

After a whole month of walking, she rarely used the chair at all anymore. She was still slow and awkward, and needed regular rest times and breaks. But she was walking more than ever and could make her way around the entire house. She'd even managed to stand long enough in the kitchen to cook dinner a few times. The slow improvement was painstaking, but obvious. And on Callum's weekly visits, he marvelled over the rate of change in her now compared with the early days of therapy. It'd been awkward for her to see him at first, after their argument in the shower. But Callum had pretended that nothing had happened between them and she'd gone along with it until she could no longer remember what they'd fought about.

Most of her time was spent alone in the house, but she'd managed to get out and about on the nearby streets most days. She couldn't walk in the sand yet, at least not long enough to make it down the pathway through the dunes. But it wouldn't be long, and she was working towards that goal every single day, with a rigid exercise and stretching routine.

She peeled a banana and stared out onto the deck. Outside, rain pummelled the overgrown garden, and in the distance, the grey waves dumped white foam along the sodden beach. The noise of the rain on the tin roof was a comforting reminder that she was safe, warm and dry in her home. Something she never took for granted.

With a bite of banana, she walked through the house. She was bored. There was nothing to do, and these days she had a lot more energy. It hadn't taken her long to get unpacked, since she hardly had any belongings. And thankfully, Hannah had left the house furnished for her. It was strange sleeping in Hannah's room, even though she'd replaced the bed with one she'd bought online and had shipped to the house. But in some ways, it helped her feel closer to the only mother she'd ever loved. She'd made it her own with a few small decorations and a painting of a horse that she'd bought when she lived in Longreach after Kevin shipped the rest of there things to her.

As she walked down the hallway, she passed the opening in the ceiling that led to the attic. An attic was unusual in an Australian home, but she recalled Hannah storing Christmas decorations and other bits and pieces there years ago. She wondered if there were still things stacked up beneath the rafters overhead. She pulled down the staircase and climbed it slowly, holding onto the hand rails to help pull herself up. She poked her head through the hole in the ceiling. It was musty and smelled of dust. The sound of rain was louder there. It didn't take long to climb all the way in and she collapsed onto her side, gasping. When she'd caught her breath, she wandered through the few neat stacks of boxes and bags that dotted the large space.

There wasn't a lot left in the attic. Perhaps Greg had gone through it already and taken whatever reminded him of his sister. But at the end, against the far wall, was a large trunk that she remembered seeing when she was a kid. At that time, the trunk had a lock on it, and she'd always wondered what was inside. Now there was no lock, and it appeared as though someone had jimmied it open recently.

She sat on the floor in front of the trunk and lifted the lid until it rested against the wall. Then, she peered inside.

There was a stack of what looked like letters, bound by a long piece of white ribbon, on one end of the trunk. The other end held a stack of photo albums. In the middle was a long package neatly wrapped in brown paper and smelling strongly of mothballs.

She coughed and covered her nose and mouth with one hand. Then she reached for the package and pulled it into her lap. It was soft and didn't weigh very much at all. Carefully, she unwrapped it and pulled back the paper to see a white dress, slightly discoloured with age.

With a gasp of appreciation, she held the dress up. It was a wedding dress. She was certain of it. And it was beautiful. Like nothing she'd ever seen before. With a bodice of lace and a long, flowing skirt. Although, the white was closer to cream, the more she considered it.

Whose dress could it be? From what she recalled, Hannah had never married. Perhaps she'd been left at the altar. Maybe this was the dress she was supposed to get married in, but never did. There was a story there somewhere. Perhaps she could ask Greg about it the next time they spoke.

With great precision, she refolded the dress and put it back in the paper and into the trunk. There were so many questions, but no answers now. It was best to put it back where she'd found it until she knew more. It was as though the dress was a person in need of its own privacy. It was the most beautiful dress she'd ever seen and she couldn't help thinking about trying it on.

The next thing she withdrew from the trunk was the stack of letters. As she took them out, she realised there was another stack beneath them, this time tied with a red ribbon that had frayed at the end. Both ribbons looked old and worn, and the paper of the envelopes had yellowed with age.

The writing on the front of the first envelope was in a sloping hand. It was written in black ink and difficult to decipher. It looked as though it read *Bronte* and something starting with an H, although it was too smudged to tell.

Whatever came below the name had been blotted out by someone. She couldn't make it out. She moved the envelope and found they were all the same. Some had the name and address blotted out, others only the address. There was only one other name, Flynn, with the last name completely obliterated. Why would anyone be so careful to remove all evidence of who these envelopes were addressed to?

She should put them back. They weren't addressed to Hannah, and they weren't hers, either. Clearly, whoever they belonged to should have them, but how would she find the person? Perhaps she could do an internet search for Bronte, although the writing looked quite old. The chances of finding anyone by that name alone were probably slim.

Then again, if she opened the letter and read its contents, perhaps it would give her more of a clue what to look for. It was preferable to return the letters to their rightful owner, and how could she possibly do that without a little more information? No, she should read at least one to see if she could garner anything useful from it.

She pulled two sheets of thin paper from the envelope. They contained the same sloping handwriting on both sides.

The writing was pushed together like the author had tried to fit as much onto each page as he or she possibly could, and some of the words were almost illegible. She leaned back against the trunk, with her knees raised and the letter resting on her thighs, and read.

——————

My dearest Bronte,

It's hard for me to believe that you're gone. The summer is over, and you're back in the city where you belong. And yet you don't belong there. You belong here, with me. And I'll never stop believing that.

Why would you leave after everything we had together?

It doesn't matter anyway because I'm going to work and save for us to be together just as soon as we can. I know your parents want someone better for you, but I'll prove to them and to you that I can be that man. As soon as I graduate, I'm going to get a full-time job and I'll save enough for us to get our own place and then we can be married.

I hope you want to spend your life with me. I sure want to marry you. But you haven't said yes yet, so I shouldn't get ahead of myself.

When you first came to Toowoomba, I was sure you'd never speak to me. You were so beautiful standing there in the park, Mick dared me to talk to you. But it wasn't hard—you were friendly right from the beginning. I knew that I'd love you forever, just like that.

Do you miss me as much as I miss you?

Mick says I'm a mess now that you're gone. We played football on Sunday, and I was tackled on the try line, which almost never happens to me. You've ruined my game. But I don't regret a thing because I would give up footy entirely if you were here with me again.

Write to me soon. I have to know that you're okay and your parents haven't banned you from speaking to me ever again. I know they were mad when they found us at the creek. Are you grounded? Is it worse than before? I wish we could speak on the phone, but I know that's impossible.

Get a message to me somehow. If you can. If I don't hear from you, I'll write again anyway. I won't stop, because I love you too much to let go.

All my love forever,

Flynn

———

Milly put the letter down in her lap. Who were these people? Bronte and Flynn were in love, but there was no date on the letter, and the stamp had been obliterated by water damage or something else. She couldn't say for certain. Someone had gone to a lot of trouble to make sure the names, addresses and any other identifying details were covered or removed from every envelope. On some of the envelopes, the stamps had been cut out with a pair of scissors. She flicked through the bundle, noting that none of them showed anything more useful.

The letter hadn't given her any clues either other than the fact that Flynn seemed to live in Toowoomba and that Bronte had visited there for the summer. Maybe she could start searching the Toowoomba area for a Flynn. It was a shame she had no last name for either of them.

She read three more letters after that. Two were from Bronte to Flynn, and one from him back to her again. All of the letters followed the same theme. They'd been torn apart so that Bronte could return to the city and to school while Flynn held on to the hope that they could be married one day. She begged him not to give up on going to university for her, that they could wait and be together after he graduated, and he vacillated back and forth between wanting to become an engineer and labouring on a local farm so they could get married immediately.

Just as she was about to open the next letter, her doorbell downstairs rang. She quickly put the pile of letters back into the trunk, grabbed one of the photo albums, and hurried as best she could down the ladder and through the house.

"I'm coming! I'm coming!" she called as she trundled along. "I'm as slow as a sloth, but I'll get there. Don't leave yet."

When she opened the door, she expected to see her grocery delivery. Instead, she found herself face-to-face with a laughing Emily.

"Did I interrupt something?"

Milly crossed her arms. "It takes me a while to get to the door."

Emily did a little dance. "Can I come in? I'm busting."

"Come on in." Milly grinned. "You remember the bathroom's on the left. I'll make tea."

"That sounds great." Emily rushed off to the bathroom, and Milly headed to the kitchen to switch on the kettle. She put the album outside, then fixed them a pot of tea and carried the tray out to the deck. By that time, she was exhausted and ready to sit. She set down the tray and collapsed into a deck chair with a sigh.

Emily joined her and poured the tea. "How are you? You look amazing. You're doing so well."

"Thanks. I feel good. I'm tired, but that's because I'm working myself pretty hard. I want to get back to normal as soon as I can."

"Is that possible?" Emily handed her a porcelain teacup decorated with pink flowers and green leaves.

"I'm not sure. I'm moving around the place okay, but the doctor says I may never be able to run or jump. We have to wait and see. He wants me not to get my hopes up. But it's hard not to be hopeful." Milly took a sip of tea. "Mmm… That's exactly what I needed."

"What's this?" Emily pointed to the photo album. "It looks familiar."

"I found it in a trunk up in the attic. I haven't looked through it yet."

"Can I?" Emily asked, reaching for it.

Milly nodded. "I'm assuming it belonged to Hannah."

Emily opened it and flipped through a few pages. "Look, there's Hannah. I don't know who these kids are with her, but she looks so young."

Milly peered over her shoulder to see a bright-eyed Hannah, with long curls brushing against her shoulders. Her hair was dark and matched her eyes. She wore a pair of jeans and a long denim top that reached almost to her knees. She was slender and pretty. Milly had never seen her like that.

"What year was it?"

Emily slipped it out of the clear pocket and looked at the back. "It says 1988."

"That's before we were born," Milly exclaimed. "Wow, she looks so happy."

They flipped through a few more pages.

"Oh, here's one of us. The three of us with Hannah," Emily said.

The photograph had been taken down by the river. Milly held a fish between her finger and thumb, a rod in her other hand as she squinted at the camera.

"This must've been right after I moved in," she said. "I look about fifteen or sixteen, I guess."

"It seems like another lifetime," Emily said. "It was the first time I remember feeling safe."

"Me too," Milly said, looping an arm around Emily's shoulders. "It took me a while to adjust, but I warmed up eventually."

"You were so grumpy at first, I was sure you were going

to kill us all in our sleep." Emily laughed as she turned another page.

"Very funny," Milly replied. "In all seriousness, though, I was so grateful."

"Me too." Emily patted her arm.

Milly leaned back in her chair and took another sip of tea. "How's the singing going? Weren't you meant to have a gig last Friday?"

"That's right," Emily said with a grin. "It was great. There were a hundred guests. It was only a corporate gig, but still, those are the ones that pay the bills. A lot of intoxicated businesspeople, but they're pretty good about clapping and dancing, so I enjoy it."

"I'll have to come and see you perform. I miss hearing you sing."

"That would be great. I've been getting more regular work lately, but it's been hard to keep food on the table." Emily set down the photo album. "I often wonder how anyone makes it in this industry. It's such a slog, and no one appreciates the artist. They all want us to work for free."

"Are you still working in retail as well?"

"Yep. Do you need any moisturiser? Because I've got you covered." Emily winked as she gulped a mouthful of tea. "Ouch! Hot!"

"I'd love some moisturiser. Thanks."

"These photos are great. You should put them somewhere safe."

Milly's mind returned to the dress in the trunk and the letters that were stashed carefully beside it. Who did they belong to? She was dying to know. "There are more albums up there. But I also found a wedding dress and some letters."

"A wedding dress? Hannah wasn't married, was she?"

"Not that I know of." Milly sighed. "You should see these letters. They're written between two people named Bronte and Flynn. They're so young and very much in love, but her parents don't want them to be together."

"Bronte and Flynn?" Emily frowned. "I don't recognise the names. I wonder why the letters are in Hannah's attic."

"Perhaps she was storing the trunk for someone, although the photo albums are hers. At least this one is. I don't know— it's all such a mystery. I'm going to talk to Greg about it."

"That's a good idea," Emily said. "You've got to get to the bottom of it because now I'm intrigued."

CHAPTER
Seventeen

CALLUM LEANED one arm out the open window of his truck, enjoying the cool of the air. His parents had called him from their cruise ship near Fiji and had asked him to check on a rural property they owned on the outskirts of Toowoomba, a city only an hour west of Brisbane.

The city perched on a high plateau — it was cold in the winter, but now that summer had arrived, it was so dry the grass that lined the highway looked dead and the road shimmered beneath the heat of the sun.

The drive to Toowoomba was a windy one. He preferred to keep the window down and smell the fresh air as he drove. It was a long way, but finally he arrived. He'd always loved the town. It was quaint and country, with beautiful green parks. Not to mention the many stunning church buildings. He drove through the city centre, marvelling over how little had changed in the years since he'd last visited. He'd spent his younger years in Toowoomba before his parents moved to Rockhampton. Memories bubbled to the surface as he drove past a white church with a tall spire where he'd attended Sunday School and had his first crush on a girl named Marcie.

The property was ten minutes outside of town, and he

figured he'd sleep in the back seat of his truck that night. It was a warm summer day, and there was no need to waste money on a hotel room when he had a decent back seat where he could curl up. He was still wrapping his head around the fact that he was a property owner now.

"We're giving it to you, darling," Mum had said during their last conversation. "We're too old to turn it into anything now. Besides, you're the one who always loved the country. It's still in our name, of course. We don't want to have to pay taxes to transfer it, but it'll be officially yours one day, so we want you to take over caring for it now."

The property wasn't worth much but he loved the idea of owning land. It gave him some understanding of how Milly must've felt when she inherited the house from Hannah, although it would've been more of a shock given her past. As one of two children in his family, Callum realised that he'd inherit half of his parents' estate one day. Milly wouldn't have expected Hannah's generosity, which made the gift that much more special.

He'd grown up in the area around the property and knew it well. But he'd never planned to move back there, and he was enjoying his time at the beach. Still, he might consider it one day. Toowoomba was a beautiful town — especially in the springtime when the flowers bloomed.

He smiled as he pulled the truck into the long dirt driveway of their property. He'd visited it many times to camp under the trees and fish in the creek. But it'd been a few years since he'd seen the place, since it was a long drive to Rockhampton from there.

There was a perfect place to park his truck beside the rundown shed where a few rusty tools were kept. He found what he needed and got to work fixing broken fencing and tidying up what rubbish had drifted onto the property. He finished with a quick run over the driveway with the whipper snipper to keep the grass short. Then he sat on an overturned log with a bottle of water and drank in large gulps as sweat dripped from his chin.

It felt good to work with his hands. He'd spent so much time in the gym in recent years, he hadn't done much physical work, and he liked it. The sound of birds chirping, the feel of the breeze on his skin, the sun on his face — it reminded him he was alive. There was nothing better than getting outside and working hard on something. Especially when the results were obvious. And they were — the property already looked neater and not as tired as it had when he'd pulled into the driveway.

The last time he'd been to the property, his fiancée had come with him. They'd brought bikes and ridden into town. They'd had a picnic under the poinciana tree by the shed. He'd been so happy. The memory of it only brought a brief stab of pain. He didn't regret the breakup. It'd been a necessary step in the right direction, but he missed the companionship. He missed the dreams he'd held in his heart for how their lives might look and where they could've been right now — perhaps married with a family on the way. But after everything that'd happened, those dreams had long ago shattered. Still, it was easier to recall the good times than the bad when he was feeling nostalgic.

The neighbour's property abutted theirs on the right-hand side with a fence that ran the length of the driveway. Beyond the fence, a horse grazed peacefully. It was bay with a white star on its forehead and white socks on each leg. It swished a black tail, sending offending flies a message to leave it alone. He watched it as he ate a sandwich he'd brought in his backpack.

As he sat there, his thoughts kept returning to Milly. She was his client, but he'd found himself feeling more for her each time they met. He knew she was fond of him, but that wasn't unusual for a client and trainer relationship — there was a bond they often developed with clients, or so his boss had informed him on day one. But that bond shouldn't be confused with romantic feelings or it would impact his career prospects. And Callum knew what that meant — mess around with the clients and you'll be fired. His boss hadn't said it that way, but he could read between the lines. He'd lost it when she'd asked for help in the shower. It wasn't professional, he could simply have found a nurse for her. But his feelings had taken him by surprise. He had to pull himself together or he'd lose his job.

Anxiety about his career trajectory brought a raft of other thoughts, unbidden, into his head. It'd been two years since his partner, Sean, was killed in a domestic violence incident gone wrong. Today was the anniversary. He hadn't wanted to be around anyone today. All he wanted was to spend some time alone to remember his friend and partner of four years. The two of them had shared a bond he'd never be able to describe to another person. They'd been there for each other, had each other's backs, shared each other's lives. But he wasn't there for Sean the way he should've been in the end. He'd gone around the building to the rear entrance, and Sean had been shot when he went through the front door. If Callum had been with him, maybe it wouldn't have happened. There'd been an enquiry and Callum had been cleared of any wrongdoing, but it'd eaten at him ever since.

He watched the horse graze while he chewed another bite of sandwich, his throat aching at the pounding memories that wouldn't stay away. They threw themselves at his thoughts like the curling waves that crashed against the sand near his apartment.

He'd started working with Brad, then broken up with his fiancée a few months later. After that, he hadn't been able to focus. He'd lost his passion for the job, and had enrolled in a personal training and rehabilitation course so he could change careers. Had he done the right thing? Perhaps, like Beth said at the time, it was his grief speaking. That he shouldn't make any big decisions until he'd had a chance to process it all. But even now, he couldn't imagine going back. He wasn't exactly happy in his new life. Would he be happy anywhere right now? But he was content, and he could finally see a chance at a future where he might learn to be happy.

The horse took a step forward and hobbled, almost stumbling. Callum set down his sandwich and climbed through the barbed wire fence. He walked to the horse, murmuring soft words that had the animal pricking its ears and watching him closely. He held up a hand and gently stroked the horse's neck. It nudged him with its nose, curious and looking for treats.

He ran a hand down the horse's leg and raised its hoof. There was something wedged in the side of it, a small rock. He used his fingers to pry it loose. It took some time to pull it free, since it'd been wedged in there with every step the animal took, but it finally came out and he tossed it over the fence and onto the road. He set the horse's hoof back on the ground, and it looked at him with interest, then walked away, this time without limping.

It felt good to do something useful, to help in some small way. Those were the things that gave him energy, that filled his bucket. He'd often wished he could find some kind of career path that wasn't so demanding, that didn't take so much of his heart whenever something went wrong. But it was no use. Even the times he'd changed course, he'd always ended up right back in the middle of another career that involved helping people, giving his heart away and waiting for it to be hurt all over again. He'd done that in the military, when he'd lost members of his unit to an explosion outside Kabul. He'd lost his partner in the force. And now he was too invested in the future success of his clients. One client in particular, Milly.

One of the reasons he'd wanted to get away from it all today was so he could think about his growing feelings for her and talk himself out of it. He was getting too involved, too connected. It wasn't healthy. He was headed for another heartbreak. This time was different, of course—the other losses had been deep friendships. But he felt more for her than that. And she wasn't dying, only moving on without him. It wouldn't be long before she no longer needed his help. The program he was being paid to provide would come to an end, the funding and the need would dry up and she'd go on with her life, without Callum. It's how things were supposed to be. It meant he'd done his job well. But he'd still be the one who was left nursing his wounded heart, and he couldn't let that happen.

He had to stop his feelings from growing before he got hurt. He couldn't keep moving cities and changing careers. He had to learn not to give so much of himself away. He cared too much. Felt too much. But he wasn't sure he could stop himself this time. It was as if his feelings for her grew against his own will.

"Hi there!" A woman's voice broke through his reverie.

He glanced up to see her marching towards him through the field, long black gumboots on spindly legs. She looked to be about forty-five years old, and wore an oversized straw hat. Beneath a pair of dark sunglasses she sported a smile.

"Hi," he said, offering her a wave.

She stopped beside the horse and gave it a pat on the neck. "I see you met Misty."

"She's beautiful," he replied. "She had a stone in her hoof. I removed it. I hope that's okay."

"Oh? Thanks for that. I'm sure she appreciated it."

"Do you live here?" he asked, looking around for signs of a house.

"Yes, just through those trees. I've got an old place I've been renovating for almost thirty years." She laughed. "It's taking a little longer than I'd planned." Her long brown hair had streaks of grey and fell softly around her shoulders.

"Renovating can be a big job," he replied. "Well, I'd better keep moving. This is my place over here," he waved a hand at his property, "and I've got some work to do before I head back to the Gold Coast tomorrow."

"So, you're my new neighbour, then?" she asked. "Oh, shoot!" She glanced at her watch. "I've got something in the oven, and I forgot all about it. It was nice to meet you. Gotta run!" As she jogged back through the field, Callum suddenly realised he hadn't introduced himself and had no idea who she was, either. No doubt they'd run into each other again. It was good to meet his neighbour, even though he still had no idea what he would do with the property. It didn't make sense to keep it. Perhaps he'd talk to his parents about selling and buying something on the Gold Coast with the money. It was time he invested in a place of his own, and the sale of the land would give him a nice deposit for a house or unit close by where he lived now.

His phone rang. The name on the screen warned him it was Beth, his former fiancée.

He answered the phone and braced for the sound of her voice. "Hi, Bethy."

"Callum, it's so good to finally connect. Why don't you ever answer my calls anymore?" she whined, the tone grating on his nerves.

"I've been busy. I have a job. You know that." He climbed back through the barbed wire and strode along the driveway to his truck. "What do you need, Beth?"

"I want to talk to you. We've got things to discuss."

"Things? Like what?"

"You know what." Her voice faltered. "Today is hard…"

He sighed. "We've said everything that needs to be said. It's time to move on. We broke up, the wedding was cancelled, and I don't know what else there is to say." He opened the truck door and pulled out a muesli bar, tore off the wrapper and took a bite.

"I need you to know how sorry I am about Sean's death."

Callum's stomach churned. "Don't… Beth. Just stop."

"Why won't you forgive me?"

"I've already been through this whole thing with you a hundred times. I've forgiven you. I've let it go. You need to deal with your own feelings of guilt because this isn't healthy, Beth."

She started to cry. The sound tore at him. "But I'm sorry. I'm sorry, and you can't just leave like that. You have to give us another chance."

"There is no us, Beth. It's over—it's been over for two years. I don't know why you can't understand that. Stop calling me, Bethy. I don't want to hurt you, but you know it's over. Please respect that."

He hung up the phone, set it on the truck seat and stared at it for a moment. Then he shut the door and retreated to the shade. He'd left the past behind, but it had a habit of creeping back up on him when he wasn't expecting it. The phone call had left him with a sick feeling in the pit of his stomach, and he'd lost his motivation to work. He sat on the ground and leaned back against a tree trunk, then stared up into the blue sky and let the memories he'd been holding at bay, pushing aside and ignoring for two years, wash over him.

CHAPTER

Eighteen

"WHERE WERE YOU THIS WEEKEND?" Milly asked.

Callum held her feet in place while she huffed her way to a sit-up. He shrugged. "I went out to Toowoomba. My parents gave me some land up there, and I wanted to see it."

"Did you go out, have fun?" She gasped for breath and did another sit-up.

He didn't respond for a moment. "No."

"Why not?"

"I don't really know anyone up there. Besides, I had some things to think about."

"What kind of things?"

He grunted. "Stop being nosy."

She pouted at that. "I'm not nosy. I'm interested."

"Uh-huh." He shook his head. "Focus on what you're doing. Your form is all over the place. Remember what I taught you. You're being sloppy."

She tightened up her form and kept going. He was such a taskmaster sometimes. She'd lost interest in this training session. She was bored with everything in her life at the moment. Everything other than the treasures she'd discovered in the attic. Speaking about Toowoomba only reminded her of what she'd found. She'd done several searches on the internet for the people who'd written the letters, but she hadn't found anything useful yet. There was no lack of information—in fact, there was far too much. Whittling it down to anything remotely helpful would take time.

"I went up into the attic the other day," she told him.

He murmured an acknowledgement, then said, "Focus."

"I'm focused," she protested. "But I want to tell you what I found."

He sighed. "Okay, stop."

She lay on her back, puffing hard.

"That's enough sit-ups. Let's take a break."

"Great," she replied, struggling to her feet with Callum's help. "You're pushing me too hard anyway."

"That's an excuse," he muttered.

"I have plenty of them," she replied with a chuckle.

"Don't I know it."

He followed her out onto the deck, and she slumped into a chair with relief. Her entire body ached. He was working her hard, but she could see the progress they were making, even if it was much slower than she would've liked. She was walking without discomfort now. It was still slow and awkward, but it was faster than before and pain free. And that was something worth celebrating — she liked to remind herself of how far she'd come every time she wanted to give up.

"I found a wedding dress in a trunk up in the attic."

He frowned. "Whose dress is it?"

"I don't know. Maybe Hannah's, but she never got married. So, now I'm dying to know the story there. I'm reluctant to call and ask Greg, since he's still mourning her loss. Would it be rude to call him?"

"Not rude, I don't think. But maybe give it a little more time." Callum was good at reading people, understanding their feelings. He was far more considerate and compassionate than Milly had ever been, and she'd come to rely on his advice.

"There were letters, too. Between two people named Bronte and Flynn. They're teenagers in love. I've read a few of the letters already, and apparently they fell in love over a summer, but then they were separated when Bronte had to go back to the city. It doesn't say what city, but Flynn was in Toowoomba, so maybe they're talking about Brisbane — which is the closest big city. Anyway, that's why I thought of it — you were talking about Toowoomba and you reminded me of the letters."

"Toowoomba, huh? That's a funny coincidence. I want to hear more, but I'll get us some drinks before we die of thirst in this heat," Callum said, heading into the kitchen. He soon returned with two large glasses filled with water and ice cubes.

Milly took a sip, and her eyes drifted shut at the feel of the ice in her mouth. It was hot outside, and the cold drink was exactly what she'd needed.

"Thanks," she said. "This is perfect."

"You're easily pleased," Callum said. "That works in my favour."

What was that supposed to mean? He'd said it with a cheeky smile playing across his lips. Even after the incident in the shower, she couldn't be certain about his feelings for her. He hadn't mentioned what'd happened since. In fact, it seemed to her he'd prefer for them both to forget it. So that's what she'd done. Maybe he'd moved on, worked through whatever he'd felt.

He'd be leaving her soon — he wouldn't be her personal trainer for much longer. She had to get used to the idea of being all alone again, but it was hard to imagine going through lonely days without him calling in to train her or texting her to check up and see how she was feeling.

"I have this vague feeling that I've been to Toowoomba,"

she said suddenly, the thought just surfacing briefly in her mind.

"Oh? You don't remember it?"

"Not really. I went into the foster system when I was three years old. And I don't think I've been to Toowoomba since then. I don't know—it's only a feeling."

"Do you know anything about your birth parents?"

"Not much. For some reason, I've never really asked about them." She frowned. Why hadn't she been curious? "I don't know their names or where they lived or anything. Is that weird?"

"It's a little weird. No one's told you anything?"

"No one." Now that she thought of it, it was beyond weird. She could've asked questions, but she'd been angry and rebellious. She hadn't wanted to know anything about the people who'd dumped her into an uncaring system like she meant nothing to them at all. Her memories of them had faded quickly because she refused to reminisce, to bring up their images in her mind's eye and remember them.

Her case officer would probably have given her at least some of the basic details if she'd asked her. But that was all so long ago — as soon as she turned eighteen, her case officer had dropped her and moved on. There was no sentimentality in the foster system. "All I remember is an image of my mother on some kind of property. There are animals around us—chooks, I think, and maybe a horse. She's reaching out her arms to me and smiling. But I'm not sure I really recall what she looks like or I've superimposed into my own mind how I'd like her to look. I was so young when they gave me up."

"And you don't know why?"

"No idea. I've always assumed they just didn't want me. But now that I'm older, I guess I should give them a little bit of grace. Perhaps they were too poor, or maybe my mother was alone. The thing is, I remember my dad too. Just a glimpse of him, standing with her in the kitchen. I don't know where we were. But I do know we were happy. I guess that's what I've resented the most — we were happy, and they gave that up like it didn't matter. I've wanted that kind of happy family ever since, but never got it. Hannah gave me something like it. She did the best she could, but it wasn't the same."

"I'm sorry," Callum said, leaning towards her. He placed a hand on her knee. "You deserved better than that."

"Thanks." She never spoke about any of this with other people. It stayed buried down deep in a part of her heart she rarely let come to the surface. She didn't like to be vulnerable, to open herself up to anyone else. It was one of the things Kevin had complained about constantly. But maybe she'd changed. The accident had changed her. She wasn't the same person she'd been before, content to go through life without any real connection to the people around her. She wanted to be real. Life was too short to be someone other than her whole self.

"Hey, maybe you could show me one of those letters. They sound interesting." He was trying to change the subject. She knew it, and he knew that she knew it. But she was relieved. She hated talking about herself and the life she had almost zero memories of living before she was abandoned.

"Okay, sure. I have a few in the kitchen. I was going to read them later, but I can read one to you, if you like."

"That'd be great. I don't have any other clients today, so we can relax. If you're okay with me staying."

Milly stood with a smile. "I'd love that."

She found the envelopes she'd stashed earlier in a drawer, then carried them carefully out to the table. She pulled the pages from one of the envelopes and smoothed it against the table.

"This one is from Bronte to Flynn. None of them have any addresses or dates, no last names. Someone has gone through all of them with a marker and blotted out anything that I could've used to track down the authors. I have no idea why, but don't you think that's strange?"

"It's very odd," Callum agreed. "I wonder what they're trying to hide. And if it was Hannah, how these people are linked to her?"

"I have to admit, I'm really intrigued. I already feel like I know these kids, although by now they must be a lot older. I'm not sure exactly, but their handwriting looks old-fashioned. At least, I think it does." She showed a page to Callum, who nodded.

"Definitely old-fashioned. No one these days uses that style of cursive."

"These days, it'd all be on email."

"True," he replied. "It's got to be at least pre-email. Probably even older."

———

Darling Flynn,

It's horrible here. Mum and Dad won't let me leave the house. I'm completely grounded after what happened in Toowoomba. I didn't think they'd take it this badly. I knew they'd be upset, but this is overkill. I hope I'm allowed to leave the house for my sixteenth birthday, but it's not looking hopeful so far.

Can you believe I'll be sixteen, just like you? Only by then, you'll be seventeen. So we won't get to be sixteen together. That would've been fun. Still, at least I can't say I'm sweet sixteen and never been kissed. I won't ever forget your kisses. I think about them all the time.

Do you think anyone else our age has ever loved the way we love each other?

I don't think so. No one at my school has any idea the way I feel about you. I tell my friends about you, and then they just change the subject and talk about crushes they have on different boys here. But it's not the same, and I can tell that right away. They don't understand what it's like to love someone so much that you feel like a piece of your soul is missing when you're apart. Or when you'd do anything just to be with that person again for even five minutes. I can't believe it's been four months since I saw you last. It's far too long.

I can't write to you often. Mum won't let me mail anything without her approval. My best friend, Siobhan, is mailing this letter for me. But she says she can't do it all the time, since she only has her allowance and her mother doesn't believe in going against other mothers' wishes. We seem destined to struggle, my love. It's how things will be. At least for now.

Do you remember when we went horseback riding together on that last day? You're a terrible rider, and I couldn't stop laughing at the way you bounced all over the place like that. I thought all country boys should know how to ride. But I guess you've been too busy on your bike and your skateboard. When you fell, I thought for sure you'd cracked your head and I was going to die of grief. But you were okay. Is your arm feeling any better? I guess it would be by now.

I kissed it all over, and you said that was the best medicine around. I don't know if you were being silly, but I liked it anyway. We can be silly together. Who cares what other people think, as long as we have each other?

I haven't smoked another cigarette or had anything to drink since we were together that night. It made me feel sick, if I'm truly honest with you. I'm sorry I can't be as cool as your friends in Toowoomba, but I have asthma and I don't think smoking is for me. The beer was pretty yucky too. Tank and Piper seemed to love smoking, drinking, using coarse language and all of those things. And I know how much you care about your friends, but I can't really feel as though I fit in. Does that matter? I hope it doesn't bother you that I'm not one of the gang. But I had fun, because I was with you. And we always have fun together, don't we?

When can I see you again? Can you come to Brisbane? I hope we'll go back to Toowoomba to visit my cousins sometime, but I don't know how soon. And I'm sure my parents will keep a very close eye on me. They're freaking out over the whole situation. I told them to stop worrying—we love each other and we're getting married. But that only made them more upset, and before long, they were talking about boarding school. So, I've stayed quiet since then. I'm hoping they'll believe me when I say I've forgotten all about you. But of course, I can't do that. I won't ever forget.

Come as soon as you can to Brisbane. I have dance lessons three times per week. Maybe we could meet there?

If you send your letters to the address on the envelope, Siobhan can get them to me at school. Unless her mother sees the envelope first, of course.

All my love and hopes for the future,

Bronte xo

CHAPTER
Nineteen

MILLY WASN'T EXPECTING the phone call when it came. She was rinsing lettuce in her newly cleaned sink, enjoying the feel of a sparkling kitchen. She'd spent the day scrubbing every square inch and rearranging everything to include her own items in the numerous and spacious cupboards. She'd never felt such a sense of accomplishment or contentment in doing housework before in her life. Owning her home gave her a new motivation.

When her phone rang, she pulled it from the pocket of the apron she'd worn around her waist all day. She wiped her wet hands on the apron and then answered without looking at the screen, instead sticking the phone between her cheek and shoulder so she could continue rinsing the lettuce for her dinner.

"Yes, this is Milly."

"Hi, Milly. It's Kevin."

She dropped the phone, and it clattered across the floor. Her eyes widened in surprise. Quickly, she set the lettuce in a bowl and picked up the phone.

"Sorry, I dropped my phone. Hi, Kevin. I wasn't expecting to hear from you."

"I'm on the Gold Coast for a wedding tomorrow. I thought maybe we could catch up for dinner, since I'm in town. What do you think? I'd love to see you."

"Uh… Okay." She couldn't think what else to say. Besides, maybe it would give her a chance to finally get some closure on the way their relationship ended. There were things that should be said. Things she wanted to get off her chest.

After she hung up the phone, she put away her dinner things — salad and a nice piece of salmon that she'd been looking forward to eating. Then she hurried to her room to get dressed. Most of her nice dresses didn't fit any longer, so she opted for one that was loose and flowing. She'd gotten a dark tan in recent weeks with her attempts in the garden and her traipsing around the neighbourhood, and the light-blue garment looked pretty against her skin.

Then she applied some makeup and was just adding perfume when there was a knock on the door. Kevin wore a white button-down shirt with a blue jacket and khaki pants. His dark hair was combed back with gel, and he looked more handsome than she'd remembered. Her heart skipped a beat at the sight of him. She should've been angry, but all she felt was a jumble of nerves twisting around inside.

He kissed her on the cheek, and she smelled his aftershave. "You look good. I wasn't sure what to expect…" he said, clearly as nervous as she felt.

"I'm doing well. I've been walking for a while now. My trainer says I'll be running again in no time, but I don't know about that. I'm happy with my progress, though." She spoke in a stilted, formal voice, as though they hadn't dated for five long years.

"Are you ready to go?" he asked.

"I'll grab my purse." She found it on the hall table, slipped her house keys into it, drew a deep breath, and spun to face him with a smile. "Ready."

On the drive to the restaurant, she saw that Callum had

sent her a series of text messages while she'd been getting ready.

Are you busy tonight?
I'm picking up some takeaway. Do you want some?
Hello?

She texted him back.

Sorry, I'm busy tonight. Kevin dropped by unexpectedly and is taking me to dinner. Thanks for thinking of me.

He replied almost instantly.

Kevin? Your ex? Seriously?

She knew what he was thinking — why would she give Kevin one more minute of her time after what he'd done? She wasn't sure she could answer that. It didn't make sense. But her anger at him had faded, and she wanted to hear what he had to say. Why was he there? Did he want her back? Was he attempting to mend the damage he'd done? She couldn't know what he wanted until she'd given him a chance to tell her, and until then, she was curious. Besides, she had a few things she'd wanted to say to him, and this was her chance to do that.

It's fine. We're having dinner. We'll talk. It'll be good. I'll chat with you tomorrow.

She waited a few moments and received another message.

Call me if you need anything.

Okay, I will.

She put her phone away and focused her attention on her ex-boyfriend. His fingers on the steering wheel drummed along to the music on the radio. He looked awkward, uncomfortable. Silence between them had always bothered him.

"How have you been?" she asked.

"Good, really good. And you?"

She chewed her cheek. Did he really just ask her that? "Well, you know…"

"Oh, yeah, of course. Sorry."

"It's fine. I've had a rough patch, but things are improving. I have a new house, and I've made some friends."

"That's great. The beach house is yours?" He glanced at her, one eyebrow quirked.

"Yep. Hannah left it to me in her will."

"Wow, that's amazing. Lucky you."

"I guess. I mean, yes, it's lucky. But I miss Hannah. I would give anything to have her back."

"Of course," he stammered. "I didn't mean…"

"I know. It's fine."

"This is awkward," he said with a half smile.

"It doesn't have to be. We can move past the awkward

stage and just be friends. Can't we?" She wanted that—she really did. There was nothing to gain by holding on to the pain of the past. She'd experienced a miracle and joy again in her life after so much pain. She had no desire to go back to that place again and wallow.

"Yes, friendship would be good."

The restaurant was set on the beach, with a deck built over the sand on stilts. It was decorated with twinkle lights that glowed heavenward, and above it, a canopy of stars twinkled back. Milly hadn't seen the restaurant before that night, but the carpark was packed. As they pulled in, she noticed there was a line of diners filing out the door and wrapping around the restaurant's wide porch. They were beautifully dressed and all waiting patiently for their tables.

"Wow, this place is popular," she said.

Kevin grunted, looking for a parking space. "It was highly recommended. Plus, it's fun to go where the party is, right?"

She remembered why the two of them had never been a good match. Kevin loved to be around the stylish people. Wherever the fun was, he had to be there, while she preferred quietness and even solitude. She'd always wondered how he'd come to be that way, growing up in a small town like Longreach. But he'd spent four years at university in Melbourne. Perhaps that was where he'd developed a taste for the partying lifestyle.

"We could go somewhere else…" she suggested.

He frowned as he pulled the car over a curb and onto a verge. "No way. This place is hopping. You're gonna love it."

They climbed out of the car and stood at the back of the line. Milly tried to have a good attitude. There were people to watch, and the night air was cool as it blew in from the ocean. She could hear the waves crashing to the shore and see dark clouds skidding across the sky. It wouldn't be so comfortable if it rained, and her back was already beginning to ache.

After they'd been there for an hour, she was beginning to

wonder if they'd ever reach the front of the line. It'd hardly moved since they arrived.

They chatted about life in Longreach, how Kevin's job was going (well, according to him), how his family was doing (more drama than he cared to relate), and how he was coping with the single life.

"I've been dating" was all he'd say about that. "What about you?" he asked suddenly. "Have you been seeing anyone?"

"In between my hospital stay, my time in rehab or my intensive physical therapy sessions, you mean?" she asked.

He mumbled something like "Never mind" and changed the subject.

Her phone buzzed in her pocket, and she took it out to read another text from Callum.

How's dinner?

We're waiting in line at Chanee's. Heard of it?

They have nice garlic prawns. You haven't eaten yet?

No, the line is huge. I'm standing here hoping it won't rain.

How's your back?

Getting pretty painful. Also, one leg is feeling weak.

You should get out of there. Find somewhere to sit.

I'll be fine.

They argued back and forth by text for several minutes. Milly did her best to pretend she wasn't having a disagreement over the phone, continuing a lively conversation with Kevin while she ignored her growing back pain and the buzzing of her phone.

Callum called, but she didn't answer. He knew she couldn't talk right now. What was he thinking? Besides, he was her trainer. Why was he texting her at this time of night? She'd told him she was fine, but he wouldn't let it go.

Milly? I'm coming down there.

She blanched. What? Why would he come to the restaurant? That didn't make sense. She was there with Kevin. He'd be furious if she left now.

No, don't do that. I'll be fine. It's probably good for me to push myself to stand for longer than usual. Aren't you always telling me to push myself?

Not like that. I'm coming down there. You shouldn't be on your feet this long. I can't believe he took you somewhere like that when he knows your health situation. And why are you even out at dinner with him after the way he treated you?

She couldn't fault him there. Kevin should've known better than to have her standing for this long. Perhaps she should just sit on the ground. That wouldn't be great for her back either, but it might be better than standing. The pain was becoming almost unbearable now. She should just sit. Or perhaps she should tell Kevin she needed to go home.

I'm okay. I can deal with it, Callum. I'll call you when I get home.

I'm coming to get you. Don't move.

She was about to speak up, to tell Kevin that she really should sit down, when he muttered something about ordering drinks at the bar and hurried off down the outside of the line of waiting diners.

"What?" she said to his back, but he didn't seem to hear her.

Great. Now she was standing alone in the line, and if she sat down, she'd lose their place. Kevin had a temper, and she had no desire to provoke him. She'd seen his temper displayed enough times throughout their relationship. But her back was hurting so badly now that she'd broken out into a sweat across her forehead. She should think about something else. Think about the sound of the waves, the cool way the water would lap against her ankles or the way it would feel if she ever got the chance to go swimming again. If only she could go down to the water's edge and jump in. That would make everything feel better. She wouldn't even mind getting her dress wet if she could float for a few minutes, take the strain off her back and cool off.

Callum seemed to have given up. He hadn't sent her another text. Maybe he'd realised just how bizarre he was sounding. He wasn't her boyfriend, but he was acting like it. Although, right at this moment, she would give anything to see his face coming through the crowd to take her away from there. She was starving, and her head was growing light from the agony in her back and legs.

Around her, people were chatting with one another. Laughing and joking about whatever was going on in their lives. No one noticed her standing there or the discomfort she was feeling. She wondered if they would notice her collapse on the floor or simply step over her and keep moving forward.

Just then, the line moved, and she took a few steps before finding a place against the wall and leaning against on it. It helped relieve some of the tension in her cramping muscles.

"There you are," Kevin said, handing her a glass of something cold.

She gulped down a mouthful. "Thank you. That'll help."

"Everything okay?" he asked, glancing around at the people surrounding them as though he wasn't really interested in her response at all.

"I'm not feeling great. My back hurts."

"Uh," he replied, still not making eye contact. "Do you think there'll be anyone famous here tonight? I've heard celebrities are spotted here pretty regularly."

She took another swallow of her drink. It was something strong with a lemony flavour. "I don't know. Maybe."

A truck pulled into the parking lot. Surely it wasn't Callum's. He'd said he was coming, but he couldn't have been serious. She frowned as she saw him climb out and jog up the walkway, ducking between waiting diners.

When he saw her, his face was a mixture of thunder and concern. He pushed through the people surrounding her and stopped in front of her.

"Are you okay?"

"I told you I'm fine." She blew a strand of sweaty hair off her face.

"You don't look fine."

"Well, thanks." She smirked.

"You know what I mean."

"Hey, what's going on?" Kevin asked, eyes narrowed.

Callum spun to face him. "You brought her here, knowing what she's been through, to stand in this line for hours in the heat. No food, no water. What were you thinking?"

Kevin's cheeks pinked. "Listen, I don't know who you think you are…"

"I'm the man who's getting her out of here. Come on, Milly. You're coming with me." His voice was low and gravelly, like a growl.

Callum slipped one arm beneath her knees and one around her back. She looped her arm around his neck, and he lifted her quickly, then carried her down the ramp and back to the parking lot.

"Hey! What are you doing, man? Milly!" Kevin shouted after them.

Milly couldn't complain. She was too busy relishing the sweet relief in her back and legs and the feel of Callum's arms around her. The immediate sense of wellbeing was overwhelming, and she fought back the urge to cry.

She leaned her head against his chest as he strode through the carpark. Then he set her gently in the front seat and buckled her seat belt. He stopped a moment, leaning closer to her face. So close she thought he might kiss her. His eyes were dark with worry, and his gaze travelled down to her lips, lingered there, then returned to meet her own. He shut the door and jogged around the truck to climb into the driver's seat.

They were silent all the way back to her house. She leaned against the cool window, enjoying the feeling of the air conditioning and the softness of the seat beneath her. She was utterly exhausted.

At the house, he carried her inside and laid her on the couch. Then he went to the kitchen wordlessly and fixed her a tray with a sandwich and a glass of milk. He brought it back to her and sat beside her while she ate.

"I'm sorry," he said after a while.

"I can't believe you did that," she said. "I'm a grown adult, you know."

He shook his head. "You have to take better care of yourself. And you shouldn't have anything to do with that man. He's bad news."

"You're acting a little possessive, Callum."

He ran his fingers through his hair in exasperation and stood to pace across the room, then back again. "I don't know why you make me feel this way."

"You're my trainer."

"I know," he replied, his eyes burning with fire.

He stepped closer, his body heat warm against her skin, and placed one hand against the couch on either side of her. "I need…"

"What do you need?" she whispered, her heart in her throat.

He leaned closer, his gaze hovering on her trembling lips. "I can't say it."

"Why not?"

"I can't." He slammed a palm into the wall and stepped back, the emotion draining from his face. "I'll see you tomorrow."

Then he was gone, the door echoing behind him. She chewed another bite of sandwich as his truck squealed away from the curb and into the dark night. Then she carried her tray to the bedroom, where she lay on the bed to finish eating and curled onto her side to sleep the deepest slumber she'd had in months.

CHAPTER

Twenty

THE NEXT DAY, Callum ran to work rather than driving. He had pent-up energy he needed to expend and only one client later that day. There was a boatload of paperwork to complete, something he often procrastinated on doing since he much preferred his face-to-face client work. He stepped into the office and removed his backpack, then drank an entire bottle of water and refilled it at the water cooler.

"Hey, Callum, can we have a chat?" Ted stuck his head through his office door, then retreated back behind the glass walls.

Callum nodded, still drinking, then carried his things to his desk. He set down the water bottle and backpack before hurrying into Ted's office.

He sat in one of the chairs facing the desk. "Sorry, I'm a bit sweaty. Was about to take a shower."

"That's fine—this won't take long. I thought we should catch up, since we haven't done that in a while, and I'm about to head out to a meeting."

"Of course. That's a good idea. I've been making progress with all my clients. I'm happy with how things are going. It's taken me a little while to adjust, but I'm getting the hang of it."

"You're still happy with your career change?" Ted linked his hands above a notepad, peering at Callum over a set of spectacles that hung low on his narrow nose.

"I guess."

"That's not particularly convincing." Ted laughed.

"Sometimes I wonder if I did the right thing. When I was in the force, I knew exactly what I was doing. I was confident. I was the good guy, fighting against the bad guys. It was clear cut. I had a way forward. But sometimes this job can be confusing. It can feel like I'm not sure which way to go, and it's hard."

Ted leaned back in his chair and crossed one long, thin leg over the other. "I know what you mean. Being a personal trainer, especially when you're working with accident and trauma victims, can be draining. Emotionally draining as well as physically. That's why I've set up a program for us all to access counselling support services whenever we need it. I'm sending around an email later today with the details of a group of counsellors. I've arranged for them to bulk bill the company if anyone on staff needs to access their services."

"That's a good idea. Thanks." Callum wasn't sure he'd ever use it. He'd had mandatory counselling on the force, especially after his partner's death, and he'd hated every minute of it. There was nothing more uncomfortable than talking about his feelings with a perfect stranger in a three-piece suit.

"You must be close to finishing up with Amelia Wilson." Ted shuffled some papers and read from one of the sheets. "Yes, it says here that you've almost used up all of the funding for her rehabilitation."

"That's right," Callum replied. "We're nearing the end of her rehab, and she's doing much better than any of us thought she would. She's walking without any aids, and she's getting close to running and jumping. She still experiences some pain and fatigue, but that's lessening by the week. I'm confident she'll have a full recovery with time." Callum drummed his fingers against the underside of his chair in a steady rhythm.

"And how does she feel about that?"

"Good, I think."

He cleared his throat, and shuffled some papers. "Could I talk to you about something personal?"

"Of course." Ted removed his glasses and set them on the desk. "Go ahead. I'm all ears."

"I've developed feelings for Milly. Romantic feelings. And she won't be my client soon, so I was wondering how you'd feel about me spending time with her on a personal level." His stomach clenched with nerves as he spoke. If he was going to lose his job, then he'd deal with that. But he couldn't ignore his feelings any longer, especially after last night. He'd caused a scene and almost kissed her.

Ted frowned. "That's not what I was expecting to hear." He stood and paced to the front of the desk, perching on the edge of it in front of Callum. "When we take on these types of jobs, it's very easy for us to develop what seem like romantic attachments to our clients. We feel compassion for them, we're concerned for their wellbeing, and those are all good things — it's part of the job. But you have to learn to separate those feelings from reality. And the reality is, just as soon as you move on to the next client, your feelings will shift and change all over again."

Callum nodded. "Okay."

"You're not the first one on staff to find himself confused over a connection to a client. It happens to us all at one point or another. But we have to remain professional. We're working within a very small community, and word travels quickly. I'd hate for you to sabotage your career path so early on. You've got a lot of potential, Callum. It would be a shame to see that all wasted because you acted impulsively on feelings that are very likely to be easily overcome."

Callum thanked Ted and left his office to make his way to the locker room in the back of the building. As he showered, washing away the sweat from his run, he thought about what Ted had said. Were his feelings for Milly only connected to his work with her? Did he feel compassion, or was it something more? He had to see her again.

Twenty-One

THE SOIL WAS hard beneath Milly's fingers. Hard and dry. But as soon as she dug beneath the surface, she found sand. She pushed her hair out of her eyes with the back of her hand and stood to her feet. It was too hot outside to keep going. She'd get back to her gardening the next morning. She'd already been for a walk and had done some exercise, although Callum was coming over later for their final training session. Even thinking about that set her heart racing.

What was up with him the previous evening? He'd texted her repeatedly, then kidnapped her from the restaurant, even though she was secretly grateful. Then he'd acted as though he wanted to kiss her and stormed out. It was all very strange.

The truth was, the more she thought about it, the more bothered she became. He was tall, strong and handsome. He'd been protective and concerned about her wellbeing. But it'd seemed more than the interest of a friend or trainer. He'd acted like a jealous boyfriend. And even though she and Kevin had dated for five years, she'd never seen him behave the way Callum did. At best, he'd been irritated if she'd inconvenienced him rather than jealous of her giving attention to another man. She was probably misreading things — he was simply angry that Kevin hadn't considered her health when he made her stand in line for so long in the heat without food or water.

She trudged slowly up the back stairs and then sat in the lounge room with a cup of iced tea to regain her strength. Every day, she felt stronger, fitter, more prepared for the future. But today, she was tired. Kevin shouldn't have taken her to that restaurant, but she couldn't hold it against him. He'd always been that way. He'd never been considerate when it came to meeting her needs. He thought only of himself, and it'd been that way for five years.

There was a knock at the door, and she opened it to see Greg, Hannah's brother, standing there with a folder beneath his arm. His grey hair was neatly combed, and he wore a checked shirt tucked into a pair of grey slacks.

"Good morning, Amelia. I hope I'm not disturbing you. I just wanted to drop off this paperwork for the house."

He handed her the folder. She gestured for him to come in. "It's good to see you. I'll get you a glass of iced tea. It's so hot today."

He stepped inside. "That would be lovely. Thank you. How are things working out?" He glanced around the living room, taking in the few changes she'd made.

She called over her shoulder as she headed for the kitchen. "It's going great. I'm loving it here. So many good memories of this place, it feels like coming home. I only wish Hannah was still here. I miss her so much."

"I know. I miss her too." He followed her to the kitchen and sat on a stool by the bench to watch her pour his glass of tea.

"How are you coping?" she asked.

He shrugged. "Some days are better than other days. I knew she was getting poorly, so it was easier to manage the grief at the time. But now that the funeral is over and life has gone back to normal, I find the grief ebbs and flows."

She handed him the tea, and they sat on opposite sides of the round dining table in the little nook between the kitchen and the deck. Milly had placed a white tablecloth with laced edging over the table. It matched the décor, given the rustic, retro feel of the place.

"That folder has everything in it to show that this place belongs to you. It's all finalised. The house is officially yours," Greg said, pointing to the folder. "But you're still welcome to call me anytime. I live about half an hour from here, and I can help with the odd thing around the place, like a blocked drain or whatever you need. Don't hesitate to call."

"Thanks," Milly replied. "I really appreciate that. I don't have anyone else to call, so I will definitely keep your number handy."

"And I hope you don't mind if I drop in every now and then. Just to see how you're doing. My wife, Joan, would love to meet you too. She's been nagging…I mean, prodding…me to ask you to dinner for weeks now."

Milly grinned. "I'd love that."

"I hope you'll find happiness here. Hannah certainly did. She loved this place." He looked around, his face beaming. "We had a lot of good times here. And there were so many children running through the halls, laughing, cooking, playing music, painting… You name it. Well, I'm sure I don't need to tell you all of this. You were here."

"I don't remember seeing you." Milly racked her brain, trying her best to recall the names and faces of the many people who used to drop in on Hannah when she lived there, but she couldn't remember Greg.

"Joan and I lived and worked in Papua New Guinea for a few years. No doubt that was when you were in Hannah's care. We've been back for a while now, though, and we're grateful to be retired and enjoying our twilight years near the beach."

They chatted about the weather and the pelicans that had been bothering Greg's boat for scraps of fish whenever he went out. They covered a range of topics, and all the while, it seemed to Milly that Greg had something more he wanted to say but couldn't find a way to broach the subject. He grew flustered whenever there was a lull in their conversation and then jumped right in with another topic.

Finally, she said, "I should get ready for my training session. It's been lovely to see you, though. I hope you'll come again."

"I'll definitely do that. And I'll send you some dates for a dinner at our place or Joan won't let me hear the end of it."

She laughed as she moved to open the door for him.

"There's one other thing I wanted to talk about before I go."

She faced him, watching as his cheeks grew redder by the moment. "Okay. What's up?"

"I know you're curious about why Hannah left you this house. And now that she's gone, I guess there's no point in keeping it a secret."

Milly waited in suspense, her skin prickling. "I've been wondering why she'd stay quiet about it. Do you know?"

"Yes," he said, scratching his chin and looking very anxious. "The thing is, I can't think of a reason not to tell you. But Hannah didn't speak up, and now I don't know what to do. So, I'm going to say it, and you can decide for yourself what to do with the information."

Now he was really beginning to worry her. What could be so dire that it would take him this long to spit it out or would cause him to be so flustered?

"Hannah was your great-aunt."

Milly was mute with disbelief. She stared at Greg, eyes wide, mouth firmly shut. After several long seconds of silence, she blurted out, "What do you mean? My great-aunt?"

"That's right. Which makes me your great-uncle. And I'm sorry I never told you that before now, but honestly I didn't know. I would've loved to have been in your life, and I'm frustrated that I was kept in the dark over it all, but there's nothing that can be done about it now, I suppose. So that's that."

"Hannah was my aunt. But if that's true, why didn't she say anything? And why was I in the foster system if I had family who could care for me? No, that doesn't make any sense."

"Please sit down, dear. Let's talk this through."

"I can't sit!" She strode to the table, spun on her heel and then went to the kitchen to fill a glass with water. She downed it in two gulps. "This is unbelievable. I have to know more, obviously. Do I have any other family? What? Where? I don't even know what questions to ask."

"Take your time and think about it. I'm not going anywhere. You can call me later to ask anything you like, although I can't promise to have the answers you're looking for. As I said, I lived overseas for a long while, and they didn't tell me much of anything, it turns out. I had no idea you existed, let alone were being fostered by my sister. It wasn't until right before her death that she decided to spring the news on me. She made me promise to take care of you."

Milly couldn't process what he was saying. Hannah was her great-aunt. That meant Greg must know who her parents were. It was knowledge she'd always wondered over but had never actively sought out. She'd told herself for years that she didn't want to know them. If they had no interest in having her in their life, why would she? And yet, something inside of her cried out to fill those gaps with names and the hole in her heart with a connection to the two people who'd brought her into the world.

"Do you know my mum and dad?"

Greg looked down at his hands where they were clenched together on the table. "I do."

"Who are they?" She braced herself, jaw clenched.

"They're two wonderful people who wanted you in their lives but weren't able to manage raising you. I can't tell you their names—not yet, anyway. I need to talk to find out what they want."

No matter what Greg said, she found it hard to believe two people she'd dreamed about for her entire life weren't able to find a way to raise her, love her, know her. They'd given her up. How could she ever forgive them for something like that?

"All Hannah told me was that your mother put you up for adoption. She always believed you'd been adopted, but then when you were around fourteen years of age, she somehow discovered you were in the foster system. That was when Hannah tracked you down and brought you home."

CHAPTER
Twenty~Two

Dearest Bronte,

The days are short, but the weeks are long. It's been an age since the summer ended and my life became a series of mundane workdays with nothing to look forward to but fixing up the old cabin at my parents' farm. I've built us a porch with a swing. Did I tell you that? It was hard work, but I managed it, finally. I'm learning a lot about carpentry. Even though Dad doesn't approve of our relationship, he's helping me anyway. He says I should never go behind the back of your parents, and I don't want to do that. But I hope they'll come around someday.

I've figured that I can come to Brisbane to see you on Thursday next week. Dad's driving down there to sell some leftover vegetables at the market. Our cattle haven't done as well this year, due to the drought. So, we're selling whatever we can to make ends meet. I've been making rocking chairs. I'm getting pretty good at them, too. But Mum is worried my schoolwork will suffer. So, I'm studying every chance I get. I don't want her to worry.

I'll come to see you outside your school when the bell rings. I'll be waiting for you. Don't forget to look for me. I'm excited to see you. I haven't heard from you in a while, so I'll just believe in faith that you've received this letter and that you still want to see me. I know you can't write me back before then, so I'll see you soon.

With all my love,

Flynn

————

Darling Flynn,

It was so great to have those few hours together on Thursday. I will treasure the memory of it for the rest of my days. Or at least until I see you again and make more memories with you. It was great of your dad to let you see me. I know he's not happy about us sneaking around. But how else can we see each other?

I loved hearing about the cabin you're renovating. It sounds amazing. It will be the perfect place for us to live when we're married. But I do wish you'd go to university first. I don't want to be the reason you can't follow your dreams. And even though it'll be hard for me, I'll wait however long it takes to be with you. Besides, I'm only sixteen, and my parents will never let me be with you before I'm eighteen. Once I'm an adult, I can do whatever I like. Or at least, I hope I can. It feels strange to imagine being independent and making my own decisions. How will we live? There are so many things we'll need to work out before then. But I have faith that we'll manage it somehow.

Where do you think you'll live if you go to uni? Maybe you can come to Brisbane to study, and we can see each other more often. I know I could sneak away every now and then. But my parents have my schedule full with dance lessons, piano lessons, athletics and hours of study. Sometimes I think it'll be easier when I'm done with school. But then other times it makes my breath catch in my throat to consider all the responsibility that I'll have to face. I know I'll be able to manage it if we're facing it together, though. Don't you think life will be easier for both of us together? It'll be happier and truer, and I don't know if I could bear a future without you in it.

When you kissed me goodbye, I wanted to hold on to that moment forever. Your lips were warm, and I could feel your heartbeat through your shirt. I've got your T-shirt right here in bed next to me. I hug it while I sleep, and I can smell you in the fabric. I wish I could kiss you right this moment. But I'm afraid I'll have to wait. Until next time.

Bronte xo

————

MILLY LAY on her back with the letters pressed to her chest and stared at the ceiling fan slowly circling above her bed. She let out a giant sigh, and her eyes slid shut. She'd never had a love like that. They were only high school kids, and teenagers were known for their crushes. But this wasn't a crush. What Bronte and Flynn shared was clearly something special. The kind of love everyone wanted. The kind of love Milly could only dream of.

She'd never wanted to let someone in past the armour she wore around her heart. But reading letters written decades earlier by two people she didn't know and would never meet — it'd broken something open in her. Maybe she should try to be vulnerable and open up her heart, if it meant sharing a love like that. It could be worth it. But would she even know how? And where would she find a man like Flynn?

There was a loud knock on the front door, and she bounded to her feet, heart pounding. She'd forgotten all about her training session. She'd gotten so caught up in reading the letters she'd brought down from the attic that she'd lost track of time.

"Be right there!" she called, quickly pulling on her running shoes.

She was still putting her hair into a ponytail when she answered the door. Callum leaned against the doorframe with a half smile, his arms crossed over his thick chest.

"We're going on an excursion."

"Um… Okay. Where to?"

"It's a surprise. You'll just have to trust me."

"Trust you? Ha!" she quipped, reaching for her mobile phone and keys and shoving them into her pockets. "Let's go, then."

Callum drove them down the coastline until he reached Burleigh Heads. He parked in a small parking lot on the side of a steep hill and climbed out. Milly followed him to a trail. He pointed along the track. "It's not very far, and there's a beautiful secluded beach at the other end. We'll probably have it to ourselves."

"I don't know. It looks steep," Milly replied, eyeing the trail warily.

Callum grinned. "You can do it. And I'll be behind you every step of the way. If you fall, I'll catch you. I promise."

They set off along the track, and before long, Milly's concerns had evaporated. She felt good. Strong, happy, care-free. She hadn't felt this way in a long time. In fact, she wasn't sure she'd ever felt this way in her life before. She'd been weighed down by the resentment she'd carried around inside her heart — it had always been there. Life was unfair, she'd been rejected, no one wanted her. They weren't conscious thoughts that she ran through often, but they hovered beneath the surface of her consciousness, ready to tear her down if she felt happy or positive about anything in her life. But something had shifted and changed in the way she felt. She'd made it through a trauma, experienced a miracle. And now she had a chance to get to know her biological family after all these years of not knowing. There was a confidence to her steps that was new.

"You seem happy today," Callum said from behind her.

She was puffing lightly. "I am."

"Care to share?"

"Let's talk when we get there. Right now, I'm focusing on

every step. I don't want to stumble on any of these rocks or tree roots."

"Fair enough. We'll talk later."

They were quiet then, striding along to the sounds of bird-song and the shushing of distant waves. They were traversing a steep hill that seemed to jut up from the coastline like a tortoise shell. It emerged from nowhere and returned to it just as suddenly. It was covered from top to bottom with a type of rainforest with green trees, vines and a coolness that belied the hot sun overhead.

Finally, after an hour of trudging, they emerged into the sunlight on a small, arcing beach. The sand was pure white, the water the clearest blue. And there was no one else in sight.

"This is spectacular," Milly puffed. "How did you know it was here?"

Callum stopped and rested his hands on his hips. "I asked around and checked it out a few days ago. Isn't it amazing?"

"I might never leave." Milly scanned their surroundings, taking it all in.

A sea eagle soared above their heads. Nearby, a fish jumped from the water and landed with a gentle plop. Otherwise, it was serenely quiet. She shucked off her shoes and socks, then plunged into the sand and relished the feel of it against the soles of her bare feet.

She hadn't been game to take walks on the beach before now. The fear of being stuck, unable to get back to her house, had prevented her from trying. But with Callum by her side, she was confident and found it much easier than she'd expected it to be.

She kicked at the sand, then splashed into the water and leaned down to flick some of it at Callum. He laughed and splashed her back. Then suddenly they were both throwing water on each other. She squealed and turned her back on him, kicking at the water with one foot. He was soaked, and so was she. She laughed so hard, she almost couldn't breathe. Then Callum grabbed her around the waist and spun her around, still laughing. He threw her into the water, and her head went under. She popped back to the surface, gasping for breath.

"Hey, my phone!"

He blanched. "Oh, sorry. I didn't think about that."

She stood to her feet and pulled it from her pocket. "I think it's waterproof." The phone looked fine. "Phew."

Then she ran at him and tried to throw him into the water, but he was too heavy for her to budge. Instead, he laughed at her and picked her up off her feet. He held her there, his eyes dark with desire as he stared into hers. Her heart rate accelerated, and her skin covered in goose pimples.

Slowly he lowered her back onto her feet at the edge of the ocean. The water reached up to her knees, lapping gently at her legs. She felt everything as though it was for the first time. The cool of the water, his warm hands on her back, the pounding of her heart against her ribcage, the heat of his breath.

"Callum... I..." The words stuck in her throat. She let her gaze wander to his lips, the heat crawling up her spine.

Then he leaned forward and kissed her. His hands left her back and cupped her cheeks, one on either side of her face. His lips were soft and yet urgent all at the same time. When he raised his head again, his eyes blinked open and he inhaled a slow breath.

"I've wanted to do that for a long time."

She smiled. "I'm glad you did."

"It's okay?" he asked.

She nodded.

He pulled her close, letting his arms encircle her. "I don't know how you feel, but I know that I want more than friendship. I want everything for us. But I understand if you're not there yet. We're in unknown territory."

"I don't know what to say," she replied, her body trembling.

"That's fine—you don't have to say anything. I've sprung this on you. But I've been thinking about it for ages, so I don't expect you to be on the same page. At least, not yet, anyway."

"I am…" she began. "But it feels so strange. We're friends—you're my trainer. I'm happy, though." And she was. For the first time in a long time, she felt completely and deliriously happy.

CHAPTER
Twenty~Three

MILLY'S WEEK had only improved every day since their outing to the Burleigh headland. Firstly, she'd received notification via email that she would receive a payout from the cattle station where her horseback-riding accident had taken place. Then, the payment had been deposited into her bank account. And yesterday, Callum had taken her to several car dealerships where she'd picked out a small blue hatchback, which was currently sitting in her garage.

It was her very first new car. She'd owned a second-hand one for years, but it'd broken down the previous year and she hadn't bothered to replace it since she'd simply borrowed Kevin's car whenever she needed to drive.

But this car was hers. A brand-new vehicle with the new car smell, leather seats and Bluetooth. She could barely recognise herself these days. And so to celebrate, she'd driven to the nearest shopping centre and gotten a haircut. Now she sported a brown bob that brushed against her shoulders. She felt young, sporty and happy. It was as if she'd become an entirely new person. Callum said he liked the style, then he'd kissed her. She couldn't quite believe this was her new reality.

Now, she was back at home, Callum was at work, and she

was searching for job listings. She'd have to find something soon or she'd end up eating into the payout she'd received since she was running low on savings. And she wanted to keep the payout for a rainy day or maybe invest it for her future. Thankfully, she'd never been a big spender and had saved most of the money she'd made over the years. But it wouldn't last forever.

She lifted the lid on her jaffle iron and pulled out a toasted sandwich with baked beans and cheese. The cheese had melted down one side, and she used a fork to push the sandwich onto a plate after it burned her thumb.

"Ouch!" She sucked on the tip of her thumb while she carried the plate to the dining table and sat, looking out over her backyard down to the deep blue ocean beyond the dunes.

It was serene and still. The wind hadn't picked up yet for the afternoon. The birds were quiet. Clouds gathered on the horizon. She opened the sandwich and blew on it, steam rising in a spiral through the air.

Beside her on the table was a stack of letters. As she ate the sandwich, she read through one of the letters where it lay open, careful not to get any baked beans on it. She was obsessed with Bronte and Flynn's story. They'd written back and forth to each other for years, and so far, she was only about two years into their correspondence.

Flynn had graduated high school, and he was attending university in Brisbane. He'd chosen to study agricultural science at the University of Queensland and visited Bronte whenever he got the chance. She was almost finished with her own schooling and was trying to decide between science, so they could be close to one another, and nursing.

———

Dear Flynn,

I'm beside myself since you're not here. I know you're probably in your dormitory, so I could call you. But I'm at home, and Dad is in a foul mood. I don't want to tempt him. Besides, I'm not sure how to say this over the phone. So instead, I'm writing you this letter, and after I'm done, I'll walk it down to the post office myself under the pretext of walking the dog.

Even though I have a lot more freedom these days, since my parents don't realise we're still seeing one another, I don't want to tempt fate. Only a few months until I'm an adult and surely then we'll finally be able to be together with no one standing in our way.

It's the strangest thing, to be staring down your future and not to be able to see a single thing. There's no light at the end of the tunnel. There's nothing in my imagination. Only you. You're all I see. But I can't figure a way forward. You have no money. I have nothing. What will we do?

If I stay at my parents' house, I'll have what I need but won't be able to see you. Or perhaps they'll change their mind now that we're older and will let me see you.

I'm going to find out. Wait right here—I'll be back as soon as I've spoken to Dad. He's in his office, stewing over something. I'm not sure what it is, but perhaps I can distract him long enough to get permission for us to date. After all, it's been two years. Surely he doesn't feel the same way he did. I'll explain that we love one another, and it wasn't just a summer fling. We've known each other for years, so many summers spent together in Toowoomba before they found out about you. They can't stay mad about that. Surely.

Well, I'm back. I can't believe I got the courage to finally confront him and ask him if I can see you. He was shocked, of course. He had no idea we were still in contact. I was polite, soft-spoken. I said we're in love and that we want to be together. That we only need his permission to see one another until I'm eighteen.

He got so angry with me. He shouted and told me I was wasting my life away. That I should be thinking about a career, not a boyfriend. And certainly not a dead-end boyfriend from some no-hope country town. That he'd let his daughter move to the outback over his dead body. And other things that I won't bother to write down because I'm too sad to put them to paper.

I don't understand his anger. I don't know why he's so opposed to us being together. And I wish I'd never said anything because now he's even more adamant about me staying in the city, going to university, and keeping far away from you. Of course, I told him that you're at UQ studying for a degree, so he says I can't attend there now. What is this obsession of his? Where does it come from?

I know you'll think I shouldn't have done it. That I should've left things as they were. But I was desperate. There's a reason I pushed him that way.

I'm pregnant.

It's early days, but I'm feeling so very sick. Every day, I think I'm going to throw up on the way to school and back again, but so far, I've managed to keep it to myself. All I can do is finish my homework and collapse in bed. Mum will notice, I'm certain of it. I've gained weight, I'm rosy-cheeked, and I'm sleeping all the time. It's bound to ring some alarm bells.

I know it's probably a shock to you, and it was to me as well. But now that the initial panic has passed, I'm excited. We can do this. Of course, I'm terrified to tell my parents. And before long, they'll figure it out for themselves. But maybe I can make it to graduation without showing too badly. I'll pretend I've simply given up on taking care of myself and am getting deliciously fat. I don't know if they'll buy it, but it might give me some time. And time is all I need. As soon as I can move out of this house and be with you, everything will be better.

I hope you're not too upset about all this. I'm doing the best that I can on my own with no one to confide in. I should've called you, I know, but I couldn't face saying it over the phone. I'm not ready to speak it out loud just yet. I'm so scared. But also happy. I can barely think straight.

Please write back soon so I can keep your words close to my heart when I go to sleep.

My love,

Bronte

———

Darling Bronte,

I'm over the moon. I can't believe it! We're having a baby? It's amazing. I wish I could leave this dorm room right this very moment and find you. I'd sweep you up into my arms and kiss you all over. If I could have my way, we'd never be apart again. But I know you're at ballet right now, so instead I'll have to write down my feelings and carry them over to you when you're done.

I'm going to meet you after class. I hope your parents are late picking you up. If they're there, I'll simply hand you the letter. If they're not, get ready for a big kiss. We're going to be so happy together, the three of us. You'll see.

I understand why you decided to speak to your father about us, and I can't fault you for it. We should've said something long ago, but it's made our lives easier to keep our secret. Now it'll be impossible to do that for much longer. If you can make it to graduation without them finding out about the baby, I think that's wise, my darling. It will be miserable for you if they take it badly, which it sounds as though they will. And I don't want anything to make you unhappy. Not ever, but especially not now, with our baby growing inside of you.

Just as soon as you graduate, I'll come over to your house. We can confront your parents together, and then I'm taking you with me. You'll be eighteen soon, and able to make your own decisions. I don't know how we'll manage, but we'll do it somehow. I still have three years of study left, but I can defer or work part-time. We won't be able to live in my dorm room, since it's for singles. But we can get married and find somewhere close to the university where we can raise our baby and live a happy, simple life. What do you think?

I know it won't be much, but we'll have each other, as you always say. And that's enough for me.

It's time to meet you now. Stay strong, my love. Everything will be better soon. I don't want us to burn bridges with your family, so let's be wise about how we manage all of this. I want only your happiness, and I know how much you love your parents and the rest of your family. I'll bring you a Mars bar too, since they're your favourite. Have you had any cravings? I wish I could be there with you for every single moment of this pregnancy. It's killing me not to be a part of your life right now. But it won't be long.

Love and kisses.

Flynn xo

Twenty~Four

THE NEXT DAY, Greg rang Milly to ask if she would visit. He said there was a family gathering for lunch, so it would be the perfect time for her to call in. His wife, Joan, was celebrating her sixty-fifth birthday. He'd wanted to invite Milly but hadn't wanted to overwhelm her. So, if she was open to meeting family, she was most welcome.

Milly hung up the phone, her palms covered in sweat. She'd fully believed that she'd never have any family. And when Hannah died, all she had left were her foster sisters. But now, she'd discovered an entire branch of people who were biologically related to her. A house full of family.

Even though the idea made her breath catch in her throat, she wasn't about to miss the opportunity to meet them. So, she quickly got dressed and hurried out to the car. She stopped at a shopping centre on the way and bought a small potted plant and a card for Joan. Then she wrote in it before driving the rest of the way to their house.

They lived in a suburb about half an hour from the beach. Their house backed onto a canal with a dock. From the street, Milly could see a large white boat anchored there. The house was large and modern, likely from the 1990s. It was built of light bricks with a red tile roof.

Milly climbed out of her car and walked nervously up the short drive. There were cars parked in every possible space along the driveway and up and down the road on either side of the house. She swallowed hard, then raised her fist to knock.

The woman who opened the door wore a colourful silk kaftan that reached to her tanned ankles. Her white hair was stylishly short, and her eye shadow matched the aqua and purple colours that dominated the swirls on her kaftan. She offered Milly a welcoming smile and swept her arms wide.

"You must be Amelia. Come in, come in! You're very welcome. I'm Joan. I've been so looking forward to meeting you."

She shut the door behind Milly, then enveloped her in a warm hug that Milly felt right down to the tips of her toes. She wasn't sure what she'd expected, but it hadn't been that. She wasn't accustomed to receiving bear hugs from total strangers. It was a little uncomfortable, but it also brought a lump to her throat.

"Come and meet everyone. We don't expect you to remember names right away. There are a lot of us, and I'm sure it's overwhelming for you."

Joan bustled down the hallway, her voluminous kaftan flowing behind her. Her feet were bare on the white tiled floor. Milly quickly kicked off her own shoes and scurried after Joan.

The living area was all white with vibrant splashes of colour in the artwork and table settings. People sat around a white dining table on white leather chairs and were scattered across a large outside deck, holding drinks and eating finger food.

"Everyone, this is Amelia!" Joan shouted, giving Milly a wink.

"Milly, actually," Milly whispered.

"Oh, sorry. Everyone, this is Milly! She's Greg's long-lost niece. Make her feel welcome." There were a few smiles and waves, some interested stares, but mostly people left her alone.

Several of the women rushed over to meet her.

"It's so good to have you here."

"Wow, welcome to the family. I didn't know a thing about you. Where did you come from?"

Milly did her best to answer their questions, although she didn't know anything more than they did about how she fit into their family. Greg soon found her and deflected the rest of the questions, leading her down a hallway to a quiet office and shutting the door behind them.

"That's a lot to deal with. Sorry about that."

"It's okay. It was nice, actually. I'm still struggling to believe those people are my family, but I have to admit it feels good to know that they are. That there's someone out there who I'm related to."

He sat behind a desk, and she sat across from him, suddenly feeling much more at ease. There was something about her uncle that gave her a sense of peace.

She sighed. "I was hoping you might be able to give me a little more information. They were asking so many questions, and I don't have the answers."

"I will. But you'll have to be patient, I'm afraid."

"Okay." Patient was the last thing she wanted to be. But she didn't have a choice, and she had no desire to be rude to Greg. He'd been so kind to her right from the moment she'd met him at the funeral. But it was so hard knowing that he had the answers, knew who her parents were, and yet wouldn't tell her.

"We should get back out there, but I wanted to give you a little break. Care for a drink?"

She nodded. "Thanks."

He passed her a glass with some amber liquid in the bottom of it. "Scotch. Sorry, I don't have any ice in here, but it's my little getaway when things become too much. I'm an introvert."

She took a sip; it burned all the way down her throat. "It's fine. I understand. I'm pretty introverted myself."

"Ready to face the hordes?"

With a nod, she stood to her feet and downed the rest of the Scotch. It didn't burn as much this time but gave her a warm feeling in her belly. "Let's go."

She spent the rest of the afternoon chatting with men, women, teens and children. There were around twenty-five people in the group, and she had no idea how she was related to any of them. What if they were brothers, sisters, cousins? She couldn't say. But one thing she was certain of—she was grateful. They were all so kind and fun. She joined in a game of cards. Then she stood on the deck and discussed yachts with three of the men, who crossed their arms and surveyed Greg's boat from a distance, remarking over the sail, the size, guessing the price and so on. She had no idea how to contribute to the conversation, but she still enjoyed it.

Finally, it was time to leave. She said her goodbyes and walked out the door with a full heart. She was far more emotional than she'd thought she would be. She'd made friends, heard family stories, and started the journey towards becoming a part of something bigger than herself. And it felt good.

When she reached home, she found Callum about to knock on her door. He waited while she unlocked then followed her inside. She offered him a drink, and they sat on the couch together. She told him all about her new family and the day she'd had. He listened in amazement, smiling and interjecting the occasional comment. She looped her legs over his, and he rested his hands on them as she spoke. She felt warm, content, accepted. She had a family. Callum cared for her. And she finally had a place she could call home. She never imagined her life could be turned upside down the way it had been, but she was finding her way to a life that was even better than the one she'd lived before.

Twenty-Five

THE FIRST THING Callum did when he arrived in his office that Monday morning was to tell his boss about the kiss. He sat at his desk, tapping the tip of his pen against the timber while he watched his boss's reaction through the glass window out of the corner of his eye. What if he was fired? Ted had already made it clear that any kind of romantic relationship with a client could mean the end of his career. But Callum hadn't hesitated to tell him. He couldn't keep working for him if he wasn't going to be honest with him. That just wasn't the way Callum operated.

Ted answered a phone call and leaned back in his chair as though he was completely relaxed with not a care in the world. The tension in Callum's shoulders eased. Maybe he was making more of it than he needed. He was an adult, and Milly wasn't his client any longer. Surely it was fine.

Even if it wasn't fine, he didn't regret it.

Recalling their kiss sent a bolt of energy through him, and he smiled to himself as he focused his attention on his crowded inbox. He couldn't regret something he'd wanted for so long. And it'd been even better than he could've imagined.

His main concern now was where she stood. Was she on the same page? They'd kissed, but what now?

He'd made plans to take her to dinner after work. And he couldn't wait.

"Callum, can you come into my office, please?" Ted called from his desk.

Callum's stomach fell. This was it. He was about to lose his job. No matter—he'd find something else. Maybe he could head back to Toowoomba and become a farmer. It was a nice idea, but not very realistic. He didn't know the first thing about farming. But he could learn, just as he'd learned how to do rehabilitation training.

He sat in the chair across from Ted, one leg jiggling with nervous tension.

Ted stood to close the door, his face solemn. "I wanted to discuss with you the topic of this morning's conversation. As I told you then, I needed some time to consider the situation. And I've done that."

"Okay," Callum replied. "I appreciate you doing that."

Ted cleared his throat and took a seat. "The situation, as I see it, is that you're in a relationship with a former client. She's no longer paying us for a service, so I don't have an issue with you pursuing that connection."

"Wow. Thank you, Ted."

"But..." Ted held up one hand. "Be careful. I don't want this to blow back on my company. I've worked hard to build a reputation as a professional rehabilitation training centre, and I don't need anything to derail that. Treat her well. Do you understand me?"

"Of course. I fully intend to do that."

"Good. And I wish you both all the best."

"Thanks." Callum stood and shook Ted's hand. "I appreciate your support."

Ted waved him off. "We've all been young and in love. We need all the help we can get to make it through."

As Callum left his office, he thought about Ted's divorce, which was still being finalised. He had a lot of sympathy for his boss, who never took out his frustrations or pain on the staff in his office. He must've been under a lot of stress, but it wasn't obvious to any of them by his demeanour at work. It would be hard to fall in love, commit your life to someone and then find that relationship torn apart years later. He had no idea what'd happened in Ted's marriage to bring it to an end, since Ted rarely spoke about it. But it must've been something big. No one got divorced on a whim. It was far too traumatic.

For the rest of the day, as Callum spent time working with clients all over the Gold Coast, he couldn't get that thought out of his head. What if he and Milly managed to overcome the odds and get married? They could end up divorced too. They could find themselves hating one another, wishing they'd never met. It could happen. He'd seen it often enough over the years. Many of the domestic disturbances he'd attended as a police officer were bound up in separation and divorce proceedings. Those people had been in love once, yet something had pushed them apart.

———

Callum pulled up outside Milly's house and carried a bunch of flowers he'd bought on the way. The sun was setting behind him, lighting the sky up in a brilliant display of gold and pink ribbons that crisscrossed overhead as they blended with the blue. Birds twittered and dived around the garden, hunting down their supper. A cool breeze blew in off the ocean and provoked a song from a set of wind chimes across the street.

He tapped on Milly's door, then waited, leaning against the doorframe, for it to open. Milly greeted him with a smile, and he leaned down to kiss her softly on the lips.

"These are for you." He handed her the bouquet.

She inhaled the scent of the flowers. They were brightly coloured — pink and purple, with sprigs of baby's breath. His whole truck smelled like them.

"They're beautiful. Thanks."

He followed her inside while she put the flowers in a vase of water. She wore a short navy dress with a thin strap around her neck and a gold necklace. She was beautiful. Her hair was short now, and he liked it that way. It was glossy and made her look cute.

"You look fantastic," he said.

She grinned. "You scrub up pretty well yourself."

"Thanks."

Their interaction was a little awkward, but they'd get better at it. It was all new and exciting, and his heart thudded against his ribcage as he helped her into the truck and shut the door behind her. She was walking so well now, no one would've guessed she'd had an accident. He could tell because he knew her so well, but most people wouldn't notice anything wrong. He was proud of her and of himself. She'd been his first seriously injured client, and he'd helped her overcome her fears and her pain to get back to a place of mobility and confidence in herself.

When he'd met her, she'd been in the dark, unable to see any hope for her future. And now she was fairly glowing.

They drove to a small seafood restaurant tucked away beside Tallebudgera Creek. They sat in the corner and bought a bottle of wine and a shared plate of calamari. The conversation flowed freely, and he watched her in awe. The way her hair fell across her face. The dimple in her left cheek when she smiled. The cute way she dipped the calamari in the aioli by twirling it right, then left, then right again.

"You never told me the reason you left Rockhampton," she said.

He swallowed a bite of calamari and reached for his wine glass. "I thought I did."

"Not really."

He sighed. "It's a long story."

"I have the time."

How much should he say? Would she see him the same way if he told her everything? But he couldn't start a relationship with someone unless he was open and honest with her. And he wanted this to be a relationship — wanted what they had to grow and to last. For him, it wasn't a short-term situation.

"I worked for five years as a detective with the police, as you know. Ten years total on the force. My partner's name was Sean. We were roommates as well as partners. We did everything together. We were like brothers."

He sipped his wine, then set the glass down again, gathering his thoughts.

"I was also engaged. My fiancée, Beth, spent a lot of time with both of us. I'd proposed, thinking that it was the next step in our relationship. She'd pressured me for years to get her a ring, and I caved. I thought it was love. But I realise now it was simply convenience. I didn't have anything to compare it with. And I was comfortable, complacent. Life was going well, even if I was in a bit of a rut.

"So, I proposed, and we had a party. Everything was going according to plan. My parents seemed concerned about the engagement, but they didn't say anything openly. And I thought it was probably normal for parents to think their son deserved better than anyone else. Now I realise, they didn't approve."

"Did you have any doubts yourself?"

He thought for a moment. "Yeah, I did. But I told myself it was just cold feet. She'd always been selfish. It was who she was. I shouldn't have settled, but it was the easiest option. And then, one day, she visited our unit, and we were all about to go out to dinner together. She went into the bathroom and left her phone on the table, and I saw a text come in. Normally, I wouldn't read her texts, but you know how sometimes you accidentally read things without meaning to? That's what happened. I looked over when the screen flashed, and there was a text that was odd."

"Odd?"

"Yeah, like inappropriate. But only mildly. So, I picked up the phone and pressed on the message. It opened, and I saw an entire string of texts from this person. A man. Someone I knew. He wasn't a friend, but I knew who he was. And it was clear my fiancée was in some kind of relationship with him."

"I'm so sorry."

"It was a punch to the gut. But more than anything, I was angry. She could've just told me she'd met someone else. We could part ways, and she could be with him. She didn't need to sneak around like that. I didn't understand it, but instead of confronting her, I wanted to think about it. Maybe I could calm down first. I was taught not to speak in anger — to give myself some space first."

"That's sensible," Milly replied. "I was never taught that. It would've helped me out so many times over the years." She laughed. "My response is always to shout in anger. But I'm going to try your approach."

He smiled. "Wait until you hear the rest of the story before you decide. So, anyway, Sean and I were out on a call the next night. There was a domestic dispute, and we were the closest unit to attend, so we decided to head that way. When we got there, we could hear the shouting. We're trained to be very cautious in domestic situations, since they're so volatile. So, I told Sean I'd go around back and see if I could find out what was going on without escalating the situation. He went to the front door, and before he could knock, the bloke saw him and shot him through the door."

"What? Oh, no. That's horrible." Milly's hand flew to her mouth, her eyes wide with disbelief.

"It was the worst thing I've ever experienced. When I heard the shot, I ran back around the front of the house as fast as I could and engaged the suspect. I took him down, then hurried to help Sean. But it was too late—he bled out. And when I looked up, I saw Beth, my fiancée, standing there."

"It was her boyfriend?"

He nodded. "They'd had a spat, and a neighbour called the cops. I've wondered ever since—if I'd just confronted her right away, maybe she wouldn't have gone over there and maybe Sean would still be alive." He swallowed hard. There was a lump in his throat, and he couldn't speak.

Milly reached across the table and laid her hand on top of his. "I'm so sorry."

"Thanks," he whispered, blinking. "I didn't mean to land all of that on you. But honestly, after the compulsory counselling I got at the station, I haven't really spoken to anyone about it. I've pushed it back into the recesses of my mind and forgotten about it as much as I possibly could. It's why I run so much — I'm trying not to think. But it all comes back to me in my dreams, so there's really no escaping it."

Milly shook her head slowly. "That makes so much sense. But you know that it wasn't your fault?"

He ran a hand over his face. "I don't know…"

"It wasn't," she insisted. "She might've gone over there to break up with him anyway. Or she might've kept seeing him. You don't know what could've happened. It wasn't your fault. It was a crime, and you had nothing to do with it."

"Thanks. You're right, I suppose."

"I am right. I know a thing or two about accidents, and sometimes they happen. You can't control everything. And there's nothing to be gained by wondering what might've been. The past isn't flexible. It's already set. We can't go back and change it. All we can do is face the future in the best way we can manage. I've learned that the hard way. I resented my accident for so long, as if I could go back and do things differently. But I couldn't. And you showed me that moving forward with hope and optimism was my only real option. Blame didn't help. Resentment didn't give me back my legs. It was you and your hope that built me up."

His heart felt as though it'd grown to double the size as she spoke. "Thank you."

CHAPTER
Twenty-Six

CALLUM SAT ON THE COUCH, and Milly had her head resting on his legs. She held a letter in her hands and waved it around as she spoke.

"I'm completely addicted to these letters. I've been reading one every day to draw them out longer. I don't want it to end. There aren't many left, and I'm dying to know who these people were and what happened to them."

"Have you asked Greg about it yet?" he suggested, stroking her hair away from her face.

"Not yet, we've been pretty busy talking about other things. But for now, I'm enjoying their love story. In a way, I don't want to know what happened because maybe it didn't work out. And I desperately want them to have a happy ending."

"Why would Hannah have kept these letters in her attic? I wonder if she knew them."

"Either the letters came with the house, or she must've known them. She's lived here so long, I can't imagine she simply forgot to empty out the massive trunk in her attic. Besides, there were photo albums in there as well, with pictures of her and all of her foster kids."

"Any photos of you?" he asked.

She nodded. "Lots. It was great to look through them, actually. Brought back a lot of good memories."

He continued stroking her hair gently. Goose pimples rose up on her arms. She loved being this close to him. They'd had such a great time together at dinner, she hadn't wanted the evening to end.

"I'll read this one out loud, if you like," she said.

"I'd love that. You've made me curious." He laughed.

"I'll read two. And that way you'll get to hear from both Flynn and Bronte."

"Okay. Sounds good to me."

———

Darling Flynn,

I'm finally done with school. My parents took me to my graduation ceremony last night, and they were pleased with my results. I'm ready to move on to the next stage of my life.

I've enrolled at UQ so I can be closer to you. My parents don't know I've accepted a position there to study nursing yet. But I hope they'll come to terms with it. After all, it's no longer their decision what I choose to do with my life. And besides, I won't even be able to complete the first semester before I have to take a break to have the baby.

I'm starting to get excited about the baby and not just nause-ated with fear. Part of that is because I got to see you last week, and you were so happy and positive. You're certain we can make a life for ourselves, and your optimism is contagious. I believe you, and I'm almost giddy with anticipation. We can finally be together, and no one will stand in our way.

When will you come? We can face my parents together.

I want us to share Christmas this year. It'll be like a dream come true. Please tell me you'll come soon so we can have our own tree at Christmas. I'll even make eggnog. It'll be amazing.

All my love,

Bronte

———

Hey Mark,

I wanted to let you know that I'm married. I know, it's crazy to announce this casually in a letter with no warning. But it was a secret, so I couldn't let you know in advance. And besides, with you studying in Victoria, we hardly see each other. I could've sent you a text or an email, but it seemed like the right thing to put it into an old-fashioned letter, since it's an important life milestone.

I'm married! I can't quite believe it myself.

Her name is Bronte. I've told you about her before. The girl whose parents were militant about her not seeing me. We met in Toowoomba before I finished high school, you might recall. I think you met her that one time when we went swimming together.

Anyway, we're having a baby in about four months' time. It's all happening at once. We got married quickly after she graduated from high school. We're probably too young. But we're determined to make it work. And with the baby on the way, we thought we should make it official, since we intended to get married at some point anyway.

Needless to say, her parents are livid. They've been ranting about how they wasted so much money sending her to private school and dance lessons. And how she's throwing her life away on a no-hoper like me (Isn't that nice? They barely know me!), and that she's going to wind up homeless and alone. They're not very encouraging.

My parents, however, have been more supportive. They're letting us have the cottage out at the farm in Toowoomba on the back of their property. We've both decided to postpone university, since she's having a baby and I've got to work to provide for us all. So, my degree is on hold for now. But I'm sure I'll get back to it at some stage.

I was hoping you might come and visit sometime, since I didn't get to have a buck's night or see you for the wedding. We had her school friends and my parents as our witnesses, and we didn't really have time to invite anyone else.

I hope you won't hold it against me, since you're my best friend. I'd wanted you as my best man, but it just couldn't be helped.

Give me a call and we'll talk.

Cheers,

Flynn

———

"Wow!" Callum said.

Milly sat up and folded away the letters, slipping them back into their envelopes, her throat tight. "They're kind of amazing, right?"

"Definitely. They were very brave, whoever they are."

"I've only got a few letters left now. I'm kind of dreading coming to the end of them. I know it'll leave me hanging. It's bound to. I suppose they stopped writing because they were finally together, so that's a good thing."

"They must've really loved each other. It's encouraging to know love like that exists in the world."

"Definitely."

"There's so much divorce, so many separations… Sometimes it seems impossible."

Milly sighed. "I know what you mean. But I think if you find a love like that, you can make it work."

"Maybe you're right."

"I don't really know. After all, I've never even seen a successful marriage close up. I don't know what happened with my parents, but they obviously gave me up, so they must not have been married. And then Hannah was always single. My own relationships have always gone bust."

Her cheeks warmed. What was she saying? She was going to chase Callum off before they'd even had a chance, and something deep inside her didn't want that. She felt a connection with him that she'd never experienced before.

"I'm sorry. I'm being a real downer about love and marriage."

"No, I get it. My parents are still happily married, but I was really wrong about my fiancée. So, I sometimes wonder if I'm going to get it right. But then, I met you. And you're so great. I haven't felt this way before."

She smiled slowly. "Really?"

"Yes, really."

"Me too," she admitted as she took hold of his hands.

He threaded his fingers through hers, slowly stroking the palms of her hands with his thumbs as he did. "I think what we have is special."

"So do I."

"Maybe we'll make it work."

He bent forward to kiss her. His lips were soft and warm, and they caressed hers gently as he moved around so he could deepen the kiss. She let go of his hands so she could wind hers around his neck and lifted herself up onto her knees. His hands flattened against her back, pulling her closer to him. Her pulse quickened, and her head grew light.

She pulled back, blinking. She felt as though she was flying when she was in his arms. She was dizzy with it, the feeling of euphoria that washed over her. She never wanted this feeling to wane.

CHAPTER

Twenty~Seven

MILLY WOKE up on her twenty-seventh birthday with a smile on her face. Sunshine slanted through the closed drapes and across her bed. She squinted at the drapes then swung her feet down to the floor, stretching as she did.

She had no plans for the day, other than dinner that night with Callum when he finished work. And since she'd been on three job interviews already that week, she planned to do nothing at all today. Or maybe she'd go to the movies on her own. She really should've thought ahead and asked someone to go with her, but everyone else would be working.

Never mind. She'd spend some time on her own and enjoy the solitude. She'd had plenty of solitude lately, but after months in hospital and rehab, she was grateful for it. She'd had very little privacy or alone time during her recovery, with a constant stream of nurses, doctors, physiotherapists and servers coming into her room. She'd never fully appreciated having her own space as much as she did now.

After a hot shower, she changed into a pair of shorts and a crop top and snuggled on the couch with a bowl of cereal and the remote control. One of her favourite things to do was to watch the morning television shows while she ate. She only let herself do it on weekends or holidays, and she laughed at an article about a dog with an unusually large litter of puppies. The animals were adorable, and she found herself missing the outback and the horses, dogs and other creatures she'd shared so much of her life with. Maybe she should get a pet of some kind.

She'd spoken to Callum about it and asked him if he was a dog person or a cat person. It was one of the most fundamental questions a new couple could debate. She was grateful to discover that although he liked all animals, he preferred dogs. A view that she shared.

There was a knock at the door. Callum stood on her doorstep holding a box in his hands, wrapped in a big red ribbon.

"Happy birthday," he said with a grin. His sandy blond hair was spiked up as though he'd walked out of the surf and directly to her house, and his brown eyes sparkled.

"I didn't realise you were coming."

"I thought I'd surprise you."

"What a lovely surprise. I was finishing up breakfast. Come on in."

She stood on tiptoe to kiss him then followed him to the couch. He set the box on the floor, and she knelt beside it. It was almost as tall as she was when she was kneeling.

"You didn't have to get me a gift."

"Of course I did. Besides, I wanted to."

"Can I open it?"

He nodded, still smiling.

She untied the ribbon and opened the top of the box. She raised herself up on her knees to look down inside and found herself face-to-face with a tiny golden puppy.

With a squeal of delight, she reached into the box and pulled the dog out. She held it against her chest, and it licked her face with a little pink tongue, its thin tail wagging.

"It's adorable!"

"He's a Golden Retriever," Callum said. "We were talking about dogs, and I thought it would be nice for you to have one. I know we'll probably have to fix the fence around the backyard, but I don't mind helping you with that. And besides, it'll be nice for me to know you have a dog here with you. He'll be a good guard dog one day."

Milly set the puppy on the ground, and he ran around sniffing everything, bounding back to her for a cuddle every few seconds.

"What will you call him?" Callum asked.

"I don't know. I'll have to think about it."

She moved up to the couch beside Callum and reached over to kiss him. He looped an arm around her shoulders.

"Thank you—he's perfect. I absolutely love him," she said.

"I'm glad, and you're welcome. Happy birthday. You deserve all the happiness in the world. I'm so proud of what you've done and how far you've come. Hopefully, this pup can bring you some of the joy you've brought me."

Her heart warmed at his words. How had she gotten so lucky to find him? She wasn't accustomed to such affection and encouragement. She wasn't sure how to respond. So instead of speaking, she kissed him again, lightly, gently. Then he pulled her to him and kissed her full on the mouth until she thought she might melt in his arms.

CHAPTER
Twenty~Eight

It's a sunny day. So hot that my feet hurt on the pavement. They're burning, so I run inside and the linoleum floor is cool. I laugh with delight and hold my arms up. There's someone there. She's pretty and young, and she lifts me up against her bosom. I lay my head on her shoulder, and I feel so safe. It's my mother, I know it is, although I hardly recognise her. It's been so long since I've allowed myself this memory. I've pushed it down so deep that it was almost lost to me. But she's here, and she's holding me, and I'm happy and secure in her arms.

Then he's there. My dad. Sometimes I wonder if I knew him at all. If he was a vapour or a part of my imagination. But he's here with us in the kitchen. Sunlight slants through the open window, sparkling on a vase filled with fresh-cut wildflowers on our white bench top. He's laughing and grabs me up in his arms to throw me in the air. I fly high towards the ceiling, then land again safely in his big, strong hands. And I don't feel scared, not one little bit.

I've never felt so safe in all my life. It's a peacefulness that fills me up like a solid foundation. I can stand on it, certain of who I am and where I fit into the world. It's a feeling that I'm not familiar with, and it brings tears to my eyes even though I know I'm dream-

ing. I want this feeling to stay with me so badly that it puts an ache in my chest.

He sets me down on the floor, then he reaches for Mum and tugs her close. He wraps his arms around her and kisses her softly, then pulls her closer still. Her hands steal around his neck, and I'm watching them in awe. I wrap my chubby arms around one of her legs and hold on tight, glad to share the moment with them and wanting to be picked up and loved on all over again.

Then she reaches for me and holds me between the two of them. "You're the cheese," she says. "And the Vegemite. You're the cheese and Vegemite in our sandwich." And then the two of them squeeze me between them until I'm giggling hard and they're both laughing along with me.

Then I wake up, and they're gone, and the cold feeling of abandonment creeps back into the emptiness of my lonely heart.

———

JONQUIL AND EMILY came to visit. They brought with them two potted plants, one a ficus and the other a lavender-coloured orchid. Milly served them a pot of tea and some scones she'd made earlier, and they all sat out on the porch together to enjoy the cool of the afternoon breeze as it drifted in from the ocean.

"The view here has always been so incredible. It feels like home," Jonquil murmured.

Emily chewed a bite of scone and swallowed. "I'm so glad you're living here. I wouldn't want the house to go to a stranger."

"It's great. And it gives me time to find the right job. I don't have to panic about not having a place to live. Hannah knew I'd need that."

"It was a pretty amazing thing for her to do," Jonquil mused, sipping her tea.

"I wanted to talk to the two of you about it, actually,"

Milly replied, working up her courage. She hadn't spoken the words out loud to anyone but Callum before now, but it was time to let her foster sisters in on the family secret. And it would help them better understand why Hannah had given her the house. "I've recently discovered that Hannah was my great-aunt."

Both girls froze, staring at her in shock.

"What? Really? How did you…? What?" Jonquil asked, eyes wide.

Milly nodded. "I know—it's a lot to take in. Trust me, I've been there. I don't know why she never said anything. I can only assume it's because she didn't have permission from my biological parents to share the details about my parentage."

"Who told you?"

"Hannah's brother, Greg. You met him at the funeral."

"Yeah, of course. And he knew?" Jonquil asked.

"He said he only found out recently. Before she died, Hannah shared with him that she was my great-aunt, and that was why she took me in as a foster kid. She'd believed for most of my life that I'd been adopted out. But when she discovered I was in the foster system, she went looking for me and took me into her home. That's why she left me the house."

Jonquil set her scone down on her plate. "Did he tell you who your parents are? Where they are?"

"No, not yet. He's meant to be contacting them to find out how they feel about it all. I don't know—it seems cruel to me. Maybe I'm reading more into it than I should. But if I knew something about your parents, I'd tell you no matter what."

"I'd do the same," Jonquil agreed. "But I suppose he doesn't understand what it's like to have no family and no idea who they are or why they gave you up. I know all about my parents, but I remember how you used to be so sad about not knowing who you were or whether anyone loved you."

"It was harder than I've ever really admitted to myself,"

Milly replied. "Now that I know I have a family, I've been doing a lot more thinking about it. And I'm remembering more about the time before... I've been having dreams, too. I think they left me on the side of the road and there was some kind of fire. But I can't be sure about it. It's so frustrating. I wish Greg would tell me more. I woke up this morning feeling so alone. I know I'm not alone, not entirely. But sometimes it feels that way."

"But you have us, and you've got Callum." Jonquil patted Milly's arm.

"I know, and I'm so grateful we've reconnected. But I wish Hannah was here, and I long for her to open up about everything. But she's gone, and she can't."

"You were going to tell us about those letters you found." Jonquil was changing the subject; she didn't like it when things got too emotional. Milly completely understood — after the way Jonquil's parents had treated her, she didn't like to talk about families or parents or to have discussions that evoked too many deep feelings. Milly had been the same way before her accident.

"Yes, that's right," Milly replied, hurrying to the kitchen to get the last few letters. When she returned, she set them down on the table. "I saved these letters to read with the two of you as there aren't many left. I'm dreading coming to the end of the story. I feel like I know them, and I care about them so much. I want them to be happy, but I may never know how things turned out for them."

———

Dear Mum,

I know you're still angry with me about the wedding. I wanted to invite you, truly I did, but I didn't think you'd come and I wanted so badly for it to be a happy day for me. I hope you can understand that. And I am happy. Truly I am. Please be glad for me. I wore the most beautiful dress. It has lace around the bodice and gemstones too. The skirt flows so smoothly, it felt like silk on my skin. I wish you could've seen me in it. I've kept it packed away to show you when we see each other next.

We've moved into the cottage out in Toowoomba. It's on Flynn's parents' property, and they've been so kind to us. They say we can live there for cheap rent if Flynn helps out around the farm. Also, he's gotten a job in town at a equipment rental outlet. The money is decent, and it means we can make ends meet when the baby comes.

It's a shame I had to postpone my nursing degree, but there was nothing else that could be done. I'm due in the middle of the semester. And Flynn had to leave university to get a job to support us. I suppose I could enrol at the university here, but I won't be able to do that until next semester at the earliest. Flynn's mother says I've got my head in the clouds if I think I'll be able to study while the baby's so little anyway.

I was glad to receive your letter yesterday. I hope it means that you've forgiven me or are getting close to it. You said the reason you didn't want me and Flynn together is that you were afraid something like this would happen, and now it has. It was never the plan to get pregnant right out of high school or to move away from you and not have you in my life. But I'm doing the best that I can in the situation I've got.

Marriage is harder than I'd thought it would be. Especially since I'm so far away from you. But we love each other, and I know we can get through this. I'm bored, since I can't work yet, and all my studies are over. I miss my friends and the life I had in Brisbane. I didn't realise how lonely I'd feel out here on a property without all of you around me. But when the baby comes, I'll have my hands full. At least that's what everyone tells me.

We don't have much money, but I'd hoped I might be able to catch the bus down to Brisbane to see you before I get too big to make the trip. What do you think? Send me an email if you can, or give me a call. Dad's still upset with me, isn't he? Will he ever get over it, do you think? Because I don't want to live without the two of you in my life.

The cottage is very quaint and big enough for us. There's a small kitchen and living room, plus one big bedroom and a very small one that might've been intended as an office or sunroom, I can't say for sure. Plus a single bathroom with a shower/bath combo. For some reason, they've carpeted the bathroom as well as the rest of the house, minus the kitchen, so there's a constant damp smell in there. But otherwise, it's very pretty. Friends and neighbours donated second-hand furniture and kitchen things, so we have all we need.

I wish I could dance again. And I'd love to go to the movies with my friends or swim at the beach. But I'm stuck out here, since I don't have a car. Flynn needs ours for driving to work and back. Occasionally I'll drop him off at work so I can have the car, but then I realise I don't know anyone or really have anywhere to go anyway.

I hope I hear from you soon.

With love, your daughter Bronte

———

Milly set the letter back on the table and looked up to see tears in Jonquil's eyes and a scowl on Emily's face.

"The poor girl," Emily said. "Her parents should've been there for her."

"I can't believe they just let her go like that, without saying anything or helping them." Milly had always wanted parents of her own, but if they treated their daughter that way when she needed them most, had she really missed out on anything?

"I wish I could give her a hug," Jonquil said.

"I don't want to keep reading now," Milly said with a shake of her head. "I'd rather pretend that everything is perfect and they have their happy ending. It's horrible knowing that all this happened in the past and I can't do anything about it."

"I wish we could talk to Hannah," Jonquil murmured.

"I've been so focused on reading these letters, I haven't considered how I'll feel if it all goes pear-shaped. With everything that's happened in my life lately, I don't think I'm ready to face that. I need to focus on something positive for a while, just until I get more stability in my life."

"I think that's wise," Emily replied, patting Milly's arm. "Give it some time before you finish the rest of the letters."

CHAPTER
Twenty~Nine

THREE MONTHS LATER, it was finally cooling off and Milly was grateful to pull on a pair of jeans and a jumper for her date with Callum. She was definitely over summer. And in Queensland summer lasted for three quarters of the year.

She'd found a job two months earlier as a dental assistant. The job was close to home, and she was able to walk or ride her bike on fine days. So far, she'd loved it — the people she worked with were kind and fun, the work itself was interesting, and she had a steady paycheck. It'd been hard at first, being on her feet for so much of each day, but her body had grown accustomed to it, and she'd continued with her weight training program. Callum was her training buddy, even though she wasn't officially a client. They simply exercised together, and she loved every moment of it. He didn't push her, but now she pushed herself, and she'd grown stronger and happier by the day.

They were going for a walk on the beach on the Cabarita headland where they'd had their first date all those months earlier. Well, it wasn't officially a date, but it was the day he'd taken her out of rehab. The day that had really turned things around in her recovery.

Callum reached for her hand as they walked up to the headland. The wind was strong off the beach, and clouds darkened the horizon.

"We probably don't have long," Callum said, eyeing the approaching storm. "How are you feeling?"

"I feel great," Milly replied. And she did. She was strong and fit and ready to tackle the steep climb to the top of the hill overlooking two long, golden beaches on either side.

The water was dark with full waves that frothed along the shoreline.

"Come on." Callum beckoned, speeding up the pace.

Milly's hair was a mess. The wind picked it up and flapped it about. She followed Callum, grateful that she was able to keep up and put one foot in front of the other. She had no pain in her back or neck. She was barely puffing. She'd worked so hard for so many months, and the work had paid off. She was free.

At the top of the hill, they stopped. By then she was gasping for air, and so was Callum. She raised her arms high and twirled around in circles, laughing. The wind was so strong, she half expected it to pick her up and carry her into the air. Instead, she felt the gentle brush of droplets of seawater on her face whenever the waves crashed against the base of the cliffs.

Callum reached for her, cupped her face between his hands and kissed her with salty lips. "You're so beautiful."

She kissed him back. "Thank you for bringing me here. It reminds me of a really happy time in the middle of the darkness."

"That was a good day," he agreed.

They stood side by side on the edge of the hill. It was shaped like a bump that jutted up out of the sand, covered in green grasses and coastal wildflowers that danced and bent under the power of the wind.

"I wanted to bring you here to tell you how much you

mean to me. These past months together have been the happiest of my life. I can't imagine living without you." He turned to face her and got down on one knee. "Will you marry me? Spend the rest of your life with me?"

She gaped at him, her heart full. "Yes!"

He slipped a sparkling diamond ring onto her finger. She felt as though she might burst. She hadn't expected the proposal—it was so soon. But she knew she wanted to marry him. Had known it for weeks now. It'd crept up on her in such a steady but confident way that it'd surprised her when she realised how she felt. She'd been afraid of commitment, of intimacy and love for most of her life. But everything had changed. She had a family now. She wasn't a nameless, unwanted child any longer. She was loved. She had a home and a steady job. And she had Callum.

————

Milly couldn't believe she was engaged. Callum had managed to keep it a secret, even purchasing an engagement ring without saying a word to her. And the ring was stunning. It had a princess-cut sapphire surrounded by sparkling diamonds. She loved it.

They sat in the truck as rain pummelled the windscreen. They'd only just made it back down the hill before the storm set in.

She stared at the ring in wonder. "How did you know what to choose?"

"It reminded me of you." He reached for her hand and kissed it. "I have another surprise."

"Really?" She couldn't imagine what else he might have planned. But she didn't care what it might be. She was deliriously happy.

"I've set a lunch date with my parents just down the road. They're waiting at a restaurant for us to join them for lunch."

Milly's heart skipped a beat. She hadn't met his parents yet. They'd been travelling the entire time the two of them had been dating.

"You didn't tell me your parents were in town."

"They got back yesterday. They've been dying to meet you, but I wanted to surprise you."

"Well, you certainly did."

"Is it okay? Can we have lunch with them?"

"I would love that." It made her nervous, but in an excited tingling kind of way. Family was something she would have to get used to, and she was looking forward to it.

They drove down the road in the pouring rain and ran into a small Italian restaurant, only getting mildly damp in the process.

An older couple sat at a table for four by the window. There was no one else in the restaurant apart from the staff. Milly felt wildly shy, as though she wouldn't be able to say a word. She didn't know how to speak to parents. She desperately wanted them to like her, but what if they didn't? Would Callum break off the engagement? She had to make a good impression.

"Mum, Dad, this is Milly. Milly, these are my parents, Frank and Gwen."

The couple stood, smiling, and shook hands with her. The man had short grey hair and a matching beard. His blue eyes twinkled as he spoke. "It's so nice to meet you. Callum never stops talking about you."

His wife playfully slapped his arm. "Now, don't go scaring the girl. I'm so glad you're here, Milly. I've been outnumbered for years. Now you can be on my side." She had short dark hair with sprinkles of silver, and her brown eyes were dark and warm as she embraced Milly.

"Thank you. I'm glad to meet you."

"Guess what?" Callum said, his voice cracking.

"What?" Frank asked.

"We're engaged!"

Frank gaped. Gwen laughed and immediately got up to embrace her son and Milly, in turn. Then Frank followed suite, with a more subdued but still happy manner. They talked and laughed, Gwen cried happy tears and kept reaching out to squeeze Milly's hand. At first Milly felt awkward and unsure of how to act or what to say, but she soon relaxed as the older couple made her feel like part of their family.

Thirty

MILLY HAD BEEN WALKING on clouds ever since the proposal the previous week. She'd had a good week at work, showing everyone her ring every chance she got. It all seemed like a dream. She'd had no hope for her life or future after her accident, and now everything had turned around. And much of that was due to two people—Hannah and Callum. She could never repay Hannah for what she'd done, since Hannah was gone. But she could reach out to Greg and the rest of her family.

She called him. He said he was close by and would stop in for a cup of tea if she was amenable. While she waited, she put tea leaves in her favourite floral china pot and opened a packet of Monte Carlo biscuits.

When Greg arrived, they sat out on the porch to watch the sunset light up the sky in shades of pink and purple.

"What a beautiful evening," Greg said before taking a bite of the oval-shaped biscuit.

"I wanted to tell you some news," Milly began. She held out her hand. "I'm engaged. Callum asked me to marry him."

"That's wonderful!" Greg exclaimed, examining her ring.

"How beautiful. I'm so happy for you. He seems like a lovely young man."

"He is," she replied. "He's more than that. I don't know how to describe him, but he's changed my life. I didn't know what love was before I met him, and now I have a reason to get up each morning. It's because of him that I'm doing so well."

"That's great," Greg replied. "Good for you. I know Hannah would've been so happy."

They chatted about her work and his boat. He and Joan were taking a three-day boat trip out to Morton Island the following weekend, and they'd been planning their menu.

"We like to eat well while we're out. It's one of the great pleasures of our lives."

"That sounds amazing."

"You and Callum should come out with us sometime. We have enough room for four. And we could swim with the dolphins over on the island. It's a pretty spectacular experience."

"I don't know. I think I would be too scared to swim with them. But I'd love to see them."

"They are pretty big. It can be intimidating."

"I like the idea, though. A trip would be nice." Getting away, out on the water, was very appealing to her after the difficulty of the past year.

"I wanted to tell you that I'm proud of how well you're doing. You've been through a lot, and you've really worked hard to get to a place where you're thriving. I know Hannah would be glad to see how much you appreciate and care for her home."

"I'm beyond grateful that she gave it to me." Milly shook her head. "It's still hard for me to comprehend that it's mine, but I'm getting there."

Greg smiled. "I'm glad to hear it because I've been hesitant to get back to you with that information we discussed. I see how well you're doing, and I don't want anything to derail that."

"You mean, about my parents?"

He nodded gravely. "That's right. Whatever I tell you, good or bad, might shake you up a bit. And you've only recently gotten back on your feet — literally and figuratively. I don't want to disrupt your progress. Maybe we should put it on hold and see how you go."

Milly considered his words with a frown. "I understand what you're saying, and I don't want to derail my progress either. But if you're able to tell me who my parents were and why they gave me up, I need to know."

Greg cleared his throat and took off his glasses. He shined the glasses with the hem of his shirt and then pushed them back onto the bridge of his nose.

Milly waited impatiently, one foot tapping out a rhythm on the timber floor.

"I spoke with your mother, and she gave me permission to tell you what I know."

"Okay." She stilled her foot, listening intently. It was as if everything in the world had fallen silent all at once. The birds were quiet, the cicadas had stopped their chirruping, the ocean was still… All of creation waited breathlessly with her.

"Your mother lives in Toowoomba. And your father is deceased."

The news hit her in the stomach like a mallet. Her father was dead? She hadn't expected that—hadn't really thought it through. Of course, it made sense. But still, it was a shock that took the wind right out of her lungs. She blinked, feeling her head go light and dizzy. "He's dead?"

"I'm sorry, honey. I know that's a lot to take in."

"It's fine—I didn't know him. I should've assumed one or both of them were gone. It makes sense. But still, I didn't really consider that option. I've been so mad at him for so long… And now I have no reason to be. He's not here." All the anger that had built up inside her all those years suddenly dissipated until it was a vapour that was gone in a moment.

"Do you want to know their names? Or is that enough for now?" He was worried about her. She could see it in his eyes.

"I want to know. Tell me everything you can." She swallowed and blinked a few times to clear her vision.

"Your parents are Bronte Harris and Flynn Wilson."

BRONTE AND FLYNN were her parents. And from what Greg had told her after that revelation, Bronte was his and Hannah's niece. According to Greg, they had been close when Bronte was young and Hannah felt very protective of her. The only thing that mattered was that she'd had a mother and father who'd loved her. And Greg assured her of that repeatedly. They'd loved her very much and had never intended to give her up.

Milly lay on her bed, staring at the fan overhead as it whirred slowly around and around. How had she missed that? She hadn't even considered the possibility that she might've been related to the authors of the letters she'd been savouring for months now. It made sense that Hannah had kept them all these years.

She didn't feel much of anything, still in shock over the revelation. She kept repeating the words over in her head… *They're my parents. They're my parents.*

And Flynn was gone. She didn't know how he'd died. After Greg shared the news about their names with her and told her how they were related and where the letters and dress had come from, she couldn't think clearly to ask questions. He'd given her an awkward embrace and then left her alone to work out her thoughts in privacy.

Now that he was gone, all of those questions bubbled to the surface one by one.

Where was her mother?

How had her father died?

What had gone wrong?

So many questions, but with no answers. There were five letters left. She'd them hidden safely away, as she'd promised Jonquil and Emily. She'd been so concerned that the story would turn out badly that she hadn't wanted to face them yet. She jolted upright, scanning the room for where she'd left them. In the kitchen. Secure in the bottom drawer beside a stack of bills to pay.

She scurried out to the kitchen, grabbed the two letters, carried them against her chest back to her bedroom and flung herself down on the bed.

With knees raised and heart pounding, she held them to herself for a moment, then carefully extracted one from the envelope. This time, it wasn't a letter, but a series of emails that'd been printed and folded into the envelope. The envelope itself was blank.

———

Dear Mum,

You haven't returned any of my letters, but I'm going to keep writing to you hoping that someday you might come around. It breaks my heart that you're not interested in meeting your brand-new granddaughter. But I'm going to tell you about her anyway. She's perfect and the sweetest little thing. If only she would sleep more, I'd be completely content.

It's hard to believe I'm a mother. I'm eighteen, and I've got an entire human being to care for. It's a lot for me to manage. Some-

times I wish I could go back to being a carefree teenager in love, without all of the responsibility. And when Flynn comes home and snaps at me because he's exhausted, it's all too much.

But then we sit outside together and rock the baby in the bouncer. And she coos and gahs, and we're in love with her and each other all over again, and everything in the world is perfect.

I know he's resentful that he didn't get to finish his degree and get a good job. The job at the store is fine—it pays the bills, just. But he wanted more. I hope he'll get it someday. Right now, there's nothing I can do other than raise this baby. She takes up every single spare moment of my day. And when she sleeps, I have so many chores to do around the house that I'm utterly exhausted. I'm not used to having no time to myself.

We've had some bad news. Flynn's mum has been diagnosed with pancreatic cancer. I didn't even know what that was, so I had to look it up. But it's bad, and it's made Flynn even more stressed than he already was. I'm worried she won't make it. She's been the only one who gave me any kind of support or encouragement. She helps me with the baby. Gives me advice. But now she's too tired and has too many appointments, so I'm on my own.

I hope you and Dad are well. Six months with a baby and I feel as though I'm only just emerging from the blur of feeding, changing, sleeping on repeat. She's getting teeth, and she's eating solids, at least a little bit. Mostly just banana and avocado mashed together right now—she loves it. But she makes such a mess when she eats, I sometimes take her outside so she can throw it everywhere while I do some gardening.

I'm trying to supplement Flynn's income by growing our own vegetables, but it's harder than I thought it would be. Everything dies, and there's not enough water — we're being told to ration it due to the drought. Never mind, I'm sure I'll figure it out if I keep trying.

I'd love to hear from you.

Your daughter,

Bronte

———

Hi Dad,

I think the white casket would be best for Mum. She would've liked lilies, too. At least I think so. I should've asked her about things like that when I had the chance, I guess. And she loved the Carpenters, so the music should be by them. I don't know what else to suggest.

I'm going to put together some photos when I get home from work. I'm so tired, I'll probably fall asleep at the keyboard. Milly has been teething, so we're not getting much sleep. (How long does this teething thing last? She's one!) Plus, all I can think about is Mum's face when she passed. I can't get the image out of my head. I want to remember her as she was before she got sick.

Anyway, I know I'm probably too late sending you this. Sorry, I've just had so much on my plate. I'll come over later and help you out as much as I can.

Cheers, Flynn

———

Dear Mum,

The funeral was lovely. It was hard to say goodbye for all of us, but especially Flynn. He's not himself at the moment. I don't know how to get through to him. He says he'll be fine, but he's got this hard shell around himself emotionally, and I can't reach him. It won't last, I'm sure. He'll come through it. But until then, it's difficult because I don't have anyone else.

You'd be proud of me — I joined a mothers' group in town. I haven't exactly made friends yet because it's only been two weeks, but I'm confident I will. The other women in the group all come from local families, so they see me as a bit of an outsider, I think. But I've always been good at making friends, so hopefully I'll find a way to wear them down.

Flynn's dad just sits on the porch staring into the distance. We go over there every night to make him eat and to tidy up a bit. Milly sits on his knee and cuddles him. She seems to understand that something's wrong. She's the only one who can pull him out of his funk, but it doesn't last. I'm worried about him. So is Flynn, but we don't know what to do. Flynn says he's going to talk to his uncle. Hopefully he will know how to handle things better than us. We've been thrown into adulthood at a very rapid pace, and sometimes it's all a bit much for us both.

Hoping to hear from you.

Love, Bronte

———

Dear Mum,

Milly is three. The time has flown by, and I can't believe how big she's gotten. Life is a lot easier. She's sleeping well and can turn the TV on for herself when she wakes up in the morning. She's potty trained and eating better, although sometimes I wonder how she's surviving on only the air she breathes and bottles of milk. The doctor says she's healthy and not to worry, but it's hard not to be a worrywart. I'm a young mum, so there's a lot of judgement, even from my friends in the mothers' group who are all closer to thirty years old.

I heard from a friend that you and Dad have moved to the UK for his work. Congratulations to him. I'm just a little sad that you didn't think to tell me, your only daughter, that you no longer live in the same country as me. I've been writing to you for three years, and yet I haven't heard from you in such a long time. I suppose I should give up, although it gives me a chance to feel as though I'm talking to my mother about the things that are on my mind. I don't even know where to send this email — maybe you're not getting my messages. Is this still your address? The next time, I'll send you a letter to your old address instead, and perhaps you'll have your mail forwarded?

Flynn has been offered a job in Brisbane. We're finally moving back to the city. I'm looking forward to it. And he says he'll try to go back to uni part-time. They've asked him to manage one of their city stores, and he's really excited about it. I'm happy for him, but I hope I'll also get a chance to study again. Although I doubt it, since with him managing a store and attending classes, I won't see much of him. Anyway, I'm going to stay positive because at least I'll be able to catch up with all my old friends. That's something to look forward to. And next year, Milly will go to kindy, so perhaps I can enrol to study nursing then.

I'll write again in a few months. I miss you and Dad. I wish you'd write back.

Love, Bronte

———

Dear Mum and Dad,

I'm writing this letter since I'm not sure you've been receiving my emails and I don't know what to do. I'm all alone in the world. It's hard to say the words, but it's true. Apart from Milly, I have no one.

You're in the UK, so maybe you don't know this, but we've had a horrible drought here for the past three years. And a few weeks ago, there was a bushfire near our farm. We were packing up to move back to Brisbane, excited to start our new life in the city together, when Flynn's dad called to say that the fire was headed our way.

I was scared. I didn't know what to do. But Flynn said I should stay put and they'd make sure Milly and I were safe. I told him to be careful and gave him a kiss, and I never saw him again.

They tell me that he and his dad died of smoke inhalation when the fire broke through the line they'd ploughed in the back field. I could see it coming, and I panicked. I put Milly in the car, and I drove away. I didn't stay like Flynn said I should. And they tell me that's just as well, since his dad's house and our cottage were both burned to the ground. We lost everything. And I lost my family.

Milly's not here. They've taken her away. They said they found her walking barefoot on the highway with the fire approaching, and I was nowhere in sight. I don't know what happened. I can't remember. All I know is that I put her in the car and we left, but then I couldn't find a way past the fire. Everywhere I turned, there was smoke and I didn't know which way to go.

After that, I recall waking up in the hospital. They've kept me here for weeks. I'm told that Milly is with a foster family and that she's happy. I think it's for the best. I don't know how to keep living. They say I'm a danger to myself and others, but I don't know if that's true. I only know that all I want to do is sleep.

I wish you were here to help me.

This wasn't how my life was supposed to go.

I won't write again. This is the last letter. I thought you should know. But I don't want to keep trying any longer. You gave up on me years ago. This is me giving up on you.

Bronte

———

Milly put both letters on the bed and let out a sob. Then she cried hard, her body racked with each sob as it became louder and louder. It all made sense — the dreams, the sense of abandonment. Bronte had been through so much and had tried so hard to pull her life together around her. Flynn had sacrificed everything for the small family. And they'd both lost it all.

She could no longer blame them for what'd happened in her life.

She didn't understand why Bronte didn't take her back again when she recovered from her injuries after the fire, but she could see how it might've happened. Perhaps she'd thought Milly was better off. Maybe she was too depressed. Whatever it was, Milly finally let go of the bitterness in her heart towards her parents. They'd done the best they could.

She cried until there were no more tears left, then padded to the bathroom to shower. Her tears mixed with the water from the showerhead and disappeared down the drain. And as she washed, the heaviness in her heart lifted. She could move forward in her life, content in the knowledge that she had been loved.

After she got dressed, she went outside to do some gardening and took the puppy with her. She'd decided to name him Sunny, since he was such a pretty yellow colour and had a happy disposition. Already he was learning to use the grass rather than the rugs in the house to do his business. And he'd only chewed one pair of her shoes, they were old and used for gardening anyway — which was why she kept them by the back door and how he'd had access to chew them.

He bounded around the backyard, chasing his own tail and the various butterflies that fluttered just out of his reach as though also enjoying the game. She dug in the soft dirt, moist from an overnight rainfall that'd drummed on the roof so loudly, she'd been woken from a deep sleep.

Callum walked through the side gate of the garden and called out her name. She stood slowly, working the kinks out of her back and neck. Her legs felt stiff from crouching and kneeling on the ground for so long.

"I'm getting old." She laughed.

He bent to kiss her. "Hardly. You have had a serious back injury, so you should be taking it easy."

She dismissed his words with a wave of her hand. "Pshaw! I've taken it easy for months. I'm sick of taking it easy. Besides, I love it out here. I feel close to Hannah, and it gives me a chance to think things through. Helps me clear my head."

They walked hand in hand up the stairs to the back porch and sat together under the shade of an umbrella she'd bought for the outdoor table.

"What are you thinking about?" he asked.

She sighed. "I read the last five letters."

"And?"

Where should she begin? There was so much to tell him. "Greg came over. He told me that Bronte and Flynn are my parents."

"They're your parents? That's a twist I didn't see coming."

"I know, right?"

He reached out a hand to rub her back. "It's a lot for you to take in. What did the letters say?"

She explained it all to him as simply as she could manage. By the end, she was choking back the tears. She hadn't been able to think, let alone talk about what'd happened without crying since she'd read the letters that morning. It was over-whelming. To finally know the truth. To understand how much her parents went through, that they would've been there for her if they could've. She knew that now.

"Wow," Callum said when she finished.

"I know. That's why I was in the garden. I've got a lot to think about. I suppose I should look up my mother now that I know her full name. But I need a minute to breathe first."

"Let's go inside and I'll make us a cup of tea," Callum suggested.

"My feet are all muddy from the garden. We got some good rain last night," Milly said, looking down at her feet in dismay. Mud reached up to her ankles. She'd shucked her shoes off when she saw how thick the mud was. She hadn't had a chance to buy gumboots yet.

"That's okay. I'll carry you," he said.

She objected with a laugh, but he scooped her up as easily and carried her into the house. She bumped her head on the doorway and rubbed it, laughing. "Ouch!"

"Whoops, sorry!" he said, bending down to kiss her forehead.

He carried her to the bathroom and set her on the edge of the bathtub. Then with a soft kiss on the lips, he left her to wash her feet while he made a pot of tea.

While she was washing the mud from her feet, she heard someone at the front door. Callum answered and let the person in. Quickly, Milly wiped her feet dry and padded out to greet them. It was Emily. Her chestnut hair was dishevelled, and her eyes were wild, darting frantically from side to side. She pressed both hands to her head.

Milly rushed to her side. "What is it? What's wrong?"

Emily shook her head. "I can't believe it."

Milly's stomach sank. What had happened? Why wouldn't Emily say it? She hated the anticipation of not knowing. "Tell me. What's going on?"

"It's good news," Emily replied, then swallowed hard. "I got a recording contract."

"That's incredible! I didn't know you were going for one. How did that happen?" Milly exclaimed.

Callum entered the living room with the pot of tea on a tray with three cups. "You got a deal? Wow. Well done."

"It's with Melon. They're one of the biggest record labels in the country. I was singing with my band, a gig in the city. And there were all these wealthy people there in their designer label clothing and such, and we were having so much fun. I love when the band just clicks, you know? And at the end of the gig, this guy in a suit came up and gave me his card. He said to give him a call. So when I did, he offered us a contract. We had to play a few more times for his colleagues to seal the deal, but we signed it this morning. I'm officially a signed artist!" Her eyes widened, and she collapsed onto the couch. "I can't believe it. I think I'm going to faint."

"This calls for champagne," Milly said, hurrying to the kitchen. "And luckily I have a bottle in the fridge that I was saving for a special occasion." She popped the cork and poured three glasses, then carried them carefully back to the living room.

"A toast, then," Callum said, raising his glass. "To Emily and her future musical success."

"To Emily!" Milly agreed, grinning heartily.

THE FOLLOWING WEEK, Greg called and asked if he could come to visit. He would bring Milly's mother with him, if she was okay with that. Bronte was coming to visit. Milly said that was perfectly fine with her, then spent the next ten minutes obsessing over how she should style her hair while her neck grew redder by the moment. She texted Callum to come over, and he said he'd be there soon.

Her heart thudded in her ears as she quickly got ready. She changed dresses three times and went back and forth about whether to use a cardigan or a jacket. The jacket was too formal. She should dress casually. After all, it was a Sunday afternoon. Who sits around their house in a suit jacket on a Sunday afternoon?

Then they were there. She heard the car pull into the driveway and hurried to the door. She stood waiting, her heart in her throat.

She opened the door after one knock. Greg stood there, mouth ajar, his fist still raised. "Oh, that was quick. I wasn't expecting… Anyway, there you are."

"Come on in," Milly said, beckoning them inside.

The woman with Greg was shorter than Milly. She sported

long brown hair that was streaked with grey. There was something very familiar about her. Milly's stomach twisted into a knot of nerves.

"Amelia Wilson, this is Bronte Harris. Your mother." Greg sounded as nervous as she felt.

"Hi, Amelia. It's lovely to meet you." Bronte's hands twisted together as though she was unsure of what to do next.

Milly smiled. "It's Milly."

"Yes, of course. That's what I used to call you when you were a baby."

Milly opened her arms for an embrace, and Bronte stepped into them with a relieved expression. Milly held on to her mother for several long seconds. Her heart felt like it was breaking into pieces. Or maybe it was opening up. Whatever was happening, it was a pain unlike anything she'd felt before.

"Let's sit," Milly said. "I'll make tea."

She brought them all a cup of tea and sat awkwardly on the edge of the couch across from her mother. "I'm glad you came to see me."

"It's long overdue, I know," Bronte said. "There's so much to explain. I'm sure you have questions."

Milly waited in silence, sipping her tea. Bronte cleared her throat. "Ahem… Well, I believe Greg told you that Flynn passed."

"Yes, and I read your letters."

"My letters?"

Milly got up and retrieved a shoebox where she'd placed the letters on the sideboard. She placed them in Bronte's hands. "Hannah kept the letters you and Flynn wrote to one another in her attic all these years. You can have them back now, if you'd like. I'm sorry—I probably shouldn't have read them, but I didn't realise they were yours. And now it feels like an invasion of your privacy."

Bronte reached out and placed her hand over Milly's for a

brief moment, her eyes warm. "Not at all. You're welcome to read them. In fact, if you'd like to keep them, you can. I'll make a copy. I prefer not to think too much about the past. There's a lot of pain in those memories for me. So, how much do you know about what happened?"

"There was a fire… And I was in foster care while you were in the hospital. Also, that your parents disowned you."

Bronte's eyes glistened. "That's right. When they heard about the fire, they came back and cared for me. But they wouldn't let me bring you home. They said you'd been adopted by a lovely family and that it was all for the best. That you'd have a much better life than the one I could give you. So, I signed the papers, and it was all over. It's the biggest regret of my life."

Milly wanted to sob, but she held the emotion at bay. "I wish you'd brought me home."

Bronte took her hands and held them as Milly sat beside her on the couch. Tears filled Milly's eyes. "I didn't understand why you weren't there. They told me you were sick. That you needed doctors to help you. But then, when time passed, you still didn't come. I thought maybe you'd died. But no one said anything, and I didn't ask. Because I preferred not knowing — I could believe you were dead and that way, you hadn't rejected me. Now, looking back, I think they told me about Dad's death, but I pushed it out of my thoughts and focused all my anger on you."

Tears fell from her eyes and down her cheeks in two slow-moving trails.

"I'm angry at me too," Bronte admitted, shedding her own tears.

And for a single moment, it was as though Milly was looking into a mirror. She saw the same heartache, the same pain, the same fears, all reflected on a face so like her own but with a few extra wrinkles around the eyes and sculpted cheekbones.

They talked then, deeply and long. Callum came in quietly and sat in the kitchen with Greg while the two women caught up on all the things they'd missed. Then they embraced once more and joined the men in the kitchen. Milly's throat ached from crying, but she felt better than she had in days.

Milly suddenly remembered something she'd wanted to ask Bronte about ever since Greg had told her the truth. "There was a wedding dress, too."

"A wedding dress?" Bronte's brow furrowed.

"Yeah, with the letters in the trunk in the attic. There was a wedding dress wrapped up in fabric. Lace bodice, jewels in the shape of flowers…"

Bronte's hand flew to her mouth. "That sounds like my wedding dress."

"Did you give it to Hannah?"

"She must've found it amongst the things that were left at my parents' place after they died. I know she was in contact with them towards the end. She was always such a caring woman. I wish I'd been here when she died. I didn't hear about the funeral until it was too late. I was overseas at the time, and I couldn't make it back."

"Would you like to see the dress?" Milly asked.

She took Bronte up to the attic. Bronte confirmed that it was her dress, and she cried a few more tears as she ran her hand over the soft fabric. "I'm so glad she kept it all these years. Wow, it still looks great. She must've kept it tucked away in anticipation that one day you'd wear it at your wedding. "

"It's beautiful," Milly admitted. "Did I tell you that I'm engaged?"

"I noticed the ring," Bronte said. "I'm assuming Callum is the lucky man?"

"That's right," Milly said shyly. "I never thought I'd find someone so wonderful."

"If he's good to you, then I'm glad. And if you'd like to

wear my dress, I think that would be really special. But only if you want to—no pressure. I know the styles have changed in the last twenty-seven years, and I did have a little bump at the time."

"I'm sure I can get it adjusted if I need to. I'd love to wear it. It would mean a lot to me." Milly beamed. She'd never imagined that she would have a family heirloom, never mind the dress worn by her own mother. It would make their wedding day even more special.

They looked through the photographs in the trunk and chattered for hours. Finally, they went downstairs to see the men.

"Thanks for being patient with us," Bronte told Greg and Callum.

"You should take all the time you need," Greg replied.

"I think we've made enough progress for one day," Milly said. "There's a lot to process."

"That's for sure," Bronte agreed.

Callum stood to embrace Milly. She leaned into his chest, relishing the warmth and safety there. This was the man she would spend the rest of her life with. And she was more certain than ever that she'd made the right choice. He seemed to sense that what she needed right now was a hug, that she'd had enough of words. She needed rest.

After Bronte and Greg left, Milly crawled onto the couch. She was physically and emotionally exhausted. It was as though she'd cried every tear she could manage and had wrung out every ounce of emotion available to her.

She yawned. "I want to tell you everything, but not tonight."

Callum tugged his phone from his pocket. "Pizza and a movie?"

"That's perfect," she said with a lazy smile. "I don't think I can move from this couch."

"Oh, one last thing before I order the pizza," Callum said. "I've seen your mother before."

"Really?" Milly sat up on the couch and rubbed her eyes with her fists. "Where?"

"She's my neighbour in Toowoomba. She lives on the farm next to mine."

CHAPTER

Thirty-Three

A YEAR LATER, Callum was out on his buck's night with his closest friends and family. He couldn't believe he was getting married the next day. Brad was his best man and had organised for them all to play golf for the afternoon, and then they went ten-pin bowling that night. But Callum had requested an early night and was on his way to Milly's house to see her before their big day.

He pulled into her driveway and climbed out, then he tiptoed across the lawn. He made his way around the house to the side where her bedroom was located and tapped on the window. The entire house was dark. She'd had a night in with her friends, but it looked as though it was over.

There was no response, so he tapped again. Then the window slid open, and Milly peered out, her hair askew.

"Callum? What on earth are you doing?" she asked, her voice hoarse with sleep.

"Sorry—I didn't mean to wake you. I just wanted to see you before I went to bed."

"Isn't it bad luck or something?"

"I don't believe in luck," he replied.

She laughed. "Wait a minute. I'll open the front door for you."

He padded around through the damp grass to the front door, kicked off his shoes, and slid inside when the door opened. Then he reached for Milly, took her in his arms and kissed her heartily. She responded in the most exciting way, deepening the kiss and winding her arms around his neck.

He withdrew from the kiss with great effort. A groan. "I don't want to leave, but I have to."

"I know. It's the last time, though. From tomorrow, there'll be no more leaving."

"I can't wait." They'd decided to live in Milly's house, since Callum's flat was so small.

"Where are your sisters?"

"They're sleeping in the guest room. Mum's here too. She has the room next to mine."

"Full house," he replied with a grin.

She sighed. "In the best possible way. My life is full, my heart is full, and tonight, my house is full."

He laughed. "I'm glad to hear it. I'll see you in the chapel tomorrow, my darling."

———

The next day, Milly rose early. Her mother was already up and in the kitchen scrambling eggs and frying pancakes. Emily and Jonquil were seated at the table busily eating and chattering nonstop about celebrity gossip, who was dating who, and how Emily's first album was going in the charts. It'd taken her six months to record and Milly loved every song.

"Are you a star yet?" Milly asked, sitting down with them at the table.

"You're up!" Emily cried.

"Did you sleep okay?" Jonquil asked, passing her a plate.

"It was fine. Callum woke me up around midnight."

"He did? I didn't hear a thing," Bronte said as she piled eggs onto Milly's plate.

"He wanted a kiss."

"Oh, that's so sweet," Emily crooned. "He's a good guy."

"The best," Milly agreed. "I wouldn't be here without him. He rescued me. He really did."

After breakfast, they got dressed. First the makeup artist and hair stylists arrived and did their magic. Then Milly donned the dress worn by Bronte when she married Flynn. It sparkled in the morning light. There was a small train and a matching veil. And when she put it all on, she felt like a princess.

Bronte embraced her gently from behind. "You look stunning. I can't get over how much the dress suits you."

"It's perfect," Milly agreed. "Thank you for letting me borrow it. I love it, but it also connects me to you. And that makes it even more special."

Over the past year, Milly had spent a lot of time getting to know Bronte. They had a different type of relationship to most mothers and daughters, but it was a special relationship. Milly had made a big effort to put the hurt of the past behind her so they could share a new bond with one another now. Living in the past had kept her bound up in her pain her for so long, holding her back from being able to form intimate relationships with other people. She didn't want to keep doing that. It kept her from happiness and enabled the people who'd harmed Bronte in the past, like her parents, to continue hurting her. And that wasn't fair to Bronte. She'd missed out on so much and suffered far more than Milly had ever imagined was possible.

They'd talked about everything that'd happened in detail. She'd shared the fact that Callum owned the property next to hers in Toowoomba, and Bronte admitted that she'd thought he looked familiar. So now, they were neighbours and often went up to their property to visit. Callum had built a small cottage on the property, and they stayed there whenever they had holiday time so they could be close to her mother. It gave them a chance to really get to know one another.

They got married in a small chapel overlooking Burleigh headland. Bronte walked Milly down the aisle and gave her away. There wasn't a dry eye in the chapel when Bronte kissed Milly on the cheek, her own cheeks wet with tears. Emily and Jonquil stood beside her as bridesmaids. The ceremony was short but heartwarming. Callum promised to catch her when she fell. Milly vowed never to take him for granted. And they both committed to remain faithful to one another until death parted them. It was everything she'd dreamed of and more than she'd hoped for.

When he slipped the ring onto her finger, she thought she might burst from joy. Then he kissed her, and all the world stood still. She was married. Amelia Montague. She loved her new name and her new husband, and was excited to start their life together.

———

Start a new series...

"Love, love, love these books!"

Ready to read start a brand new series? *The Waratah Inn* is Lilly Mirren's bestselling heartwarming women's fiction series. Buy the first book in this series!

Want to find out about all of my new releases? You can get on my VIP reader list by subscribing to my newsletter and you'll also get a free book.

WOMEN'S FICTION

CORAL ISLAND SERIES

The Island

After twenty five years of marriage and decades caring for her two children, on the evening of their vow renewal, her husband shocks her with the news that he's leaving her.

The Beach Cottage

Beatrice is speechless. It's something she never expected — a secret daughter. She and Aidan have only just renewed their romance, after decades apart, and he never mentioned a child. Did he know she existed?

The Blue Shoal Inn

Taya's inn is in trouble. Her father has built a fancy new resort in Blue Shoal and hired a handsome stranger to manage it. When the stranger offers to buy her inn and merge it with the resort, she wants to hate him but when he rescues a stray dog her feelings for him change.

Island Weddings

Charmaine moves to Coral Island and lands a job working at a local florist shop. It seems as though the entire island has caught wedding fever, with weddings planned every weekend. It's a good opportunity for her to get to know the locals, but what she doesn't expect is to be thrown into the middle of a family drama.

The Island Bookshop

Evie's book club friends are the people in the world she relies on most. But when one of the newer members finds herself confronted with her past, the rest of the club will do what they can to help, endangering the existence of the bookshop without realising it.

An Island Reunion

It's been thirty five years since the friends graduated from Coral Island State Primary School and the class is returning to the island to celebrate.

THE WARATAH INN SERIES

The Waratah Inn

Wrested back to Cabarita Beach by her grandmother's sudden death, Kate Summer discovers a mystery buried in the past that changes everything.

One Summer in Italy

Reeda leaves the Waratah Inn and returns to Sydney, her husband, and her thriving interior design business, only to find her marriage in tatters. She's lost sight of what she wants in life and can't recognise the person she's become.

The Summer Sisters

Set against the golden sands and crystal clear waters of Cabarita Beach three sisters inherit an inn and discover a mystery about their grandmother's past that changes everything they thought they knew about their family...

Christmas at The Waratah Inn

Liz Cranwell is divorced and alone at Christmas. When her friends convince her to holiday at The Waratah Inn, she's dreading her first Christmas on her own. Instead she discovers that strangers can be the balm to heal the wounds of a lonely heart in this heartwarming Christmas story.

EMERALD COVE SERIES

Cottage on Oceanview Lane

When a renowned book editor returns to her roots, she rediscovers her strength & her passion in this heartwarming novel.

Seaside Manor Bed & Breakfast

The Seaside Manor Bed and Breakfast has been an institution in Emerald Cove for as long as anyone can remember. But things are changing and Diana is nervous about what the future might hold for her and her husband, not to mention the historic business.

Bungalow on Pelican Way

Moving to the Cove gave Rebecca De Vries a place to hide from her abusive ex. Now that he's in jail, she can get back to living her life as a police officer in her adopted hometown working alongside her intractable but very attractive boss, Franklin.

Chalet on Cliffside Drive

At forty-four years of age, Ben Silver thought he'd never find love. When he moves to Emerald Cove, he does it to support his birth mother, Diana, after her husband's sudden death. But then he meets Vicky.

An Emerald Cove Christmas

The Flannigan family has been through a lot together. They've grown and changed over the years and now have a blended and extended family that doesn't always see eye to eye. But this Christmas they'll learn that love can overcome all of the pain and differences of the past in this inspiring Christmas tale.

MYSTERIES

White Picket Lies

Fighting the demons of her past Toni finds herself in the midst of a second marriage breakdown at forty seven years of age. She struggles to keep depression at bay while doing her best to raise a wayward teenaged son and uncover the identity of the killer.

In this small town investigation, it's only a matter of time until friends and neighbours turn on each other.

HISTORICAL FICTION (WRITING AS BRONWEN PRATLEY)

Beyond the Crushing Waves

An emotional standalone historical saga. Two children plucked from poverty & forcibly deported from the UK to Australia. Inspired by true events. An unforgettable tale of loss, love, redemption & new beginnings.

Under a Sunburnt Sky

Inspired by a true story. Jan Kostanski is a normal Catholic boy in Warsaw when the nazis invade. He's separated from his neighbours, a Jewish family who he considers kin, by the ghetto wall. Jan and his mother decide that they will do whatever it takes to save their Jewish friends from certain death. The unforgettable tale of an everyday family's fight against evil, and the unbreakable bonds of their love.

Lilly Mirren is an Amazon top 20, Audible top 15 and *USA Today* Bestselling author who has sold over two million copies of her books worldwide. She lives in Brisbane, Australia with her husband and three children.

Her books combine heartwarming storylines with realistic characters readers see as friends.

Her debut series, *The Waratah Inn*, set in the delightful Cabarita Beach, hit the *USA Today* Bestseller list and since then, has touched the hearts of hundreds of thousands of readers across the globe.